HOOKED
ON HIS
Thuggish
WAYS
2

A NOVEL BY

PRENISHA AJA

Royalty Publishing House is now accepting manuscripts from aspiring or experienced urban romance authors!

WHAT MAY PLACE YOU ABOVE THE REST:

Heroes who are the ultimate book bae: strong-willed, maybe a little rough around the edges but willing to risk it all for the woman he loves.

Heroines who are the ultimate match: the girl next door type, not perfect - has her faults but is still a decent person. One who is willing to risk it all for the man she loves.

The rest is up to you! Just be creative, think out of the box, keep it sexy and intriguing!

If you'd like to join the Royal family, send us the first 15K words (60 pages) of your completed manuscript to submissions@royaltypublishing-house.com

SYNOPSIS

The drama only gets deeper as we dig into this suspenseful story. The ending left everyone wondering who was behind the wheel of the car and is Keisha ok.

Jaxsyn is now out for revenge and the only thing he can think about is taking Whoodie out. He also finds himself having a hard time coping with everything going on which results in him pushing the one person that only wants to be there for him away.

Kaizlyn finds herself deep off in her feelings when Jaxsyn gives her the cold shoulder but the question is, how long will that last? Will Jaxsyn come back to his senses or will someone from her past catch her eye?

In this drama filled story, revenge is something that so many are seeking no matter the cost.

Lies and drama seem to follow as secrets start to become too hard to hold in, and the past finds itself knocking on the front door, demanding attention.

DEDICATION

This book is dedicated to everyone who is continuously supporting me through this amazing journey. I still can't believe that I'm a published author.

Also, to my friends (Hydiea, Vee, and Kaa), thank you for the extra push. Every last one of y'all are bomb and it's only up from here. And last but not least, my mother, Regina, who is book crazy. She has supported every last one of my releases and I am forever grateful. She goes above and beyond to push my books to others. Thank you Mommy. I love you.

Thank you God for it all. Without you I would be nothing.

Jaxsyn

"You ready to do this?" Ace asked me as we sat in an all-black Escalade that we had rented. I had told myself that if my sister wasn't at school that I was going to run up in his shit, and that's exactly what I was about to do. I had already wasted too much time, trying to give her time.

"Hell yeah. I'm about to go get her ass up out of there even if she doesn't want to come." I cocked my gun. I then got out of the car and ran smoothly up to the door, making sure to check my surroundings.

"5,4,3,2,1," I counted down slowly. I then kicked the door in with my gun raised in the air and Ace right behind me.

We had sent our boys out to get the scoop and to find out where that nigga Whoodie laid his head. They later came to me letting me know that he stayed with his peoples and after digging through their mail, they also found out their names too.

I mean, to be honest, if it came down to it, I would take them out to just to prove my point. I wasn't bullshitting no more. I had already been too lenient and look at what the fuck happened. So if it took me having to kill more of his people to get an understanding, then so fucking be it.

With my gun ready to go, the first thing that caught my eye was the blood on the carpet. Some of it was beginning to soak into the carpet and dry up, but I could tell that it was fresh blood and all I could do was begin to think about my sister.

My stomach began to knot up and I had this terrible feeling in my gut that I wanted to go away. Like that ill feeling you get that makes you feel empty on the inside. I literally had to pause and lean up against the wall to catch my breath.

"You good bro?" Ace looked from the blood to me.

"Ion even know," I replied.

Shaking my head, I looked at Ace and he was wearing the same expression as me. We both looked like we were sick to our stomachs and the last thing we wanted to do was accept that something terrible had happened to my sister. I knew I didn't. I didn't want to believe that it was my sister's blood on the floor. Period.

Fuck, I sighed. I then took a really deep breath as I continued to look throughout the house, but there were no signs of my sister or Whoodie.

Now my heart was damn near pounding out of my chest because I was over this shit. I was no longer up for the bullshit ass antics.

"What you want to do? Say the word and I'm on it," Ace asked as he stood behind me.

I was currently standing in the middle of the floor with my hands on top of my head as I looked up at the ceiling.

I was so used to keeping my emotions under control, and now I was slowly losing that battle. My thoughts weren't making anything easier for me because the more I thought about my sister, the angrier I got. I wanted to release this anger on somebody. Anybody.

"I don't fucking know. Fuck," I expressed as I turned and punched a hole in the wall. My frustrations were at an all-time high and I knew nothing would actually fix it besides my sister being in my presence.

Shaking my hand up and down, I tried to shake off the slight pain that I felt as I looked at Ace.

"This shit is fucking with me because I don't know if my fucking sister is ok. I want to find that nigga now. Right fucking now," I roared.

I was no longer taking things easy. That was getting me nowhere. I was about to get some shit poppin', even if that meant going to every-body's house that I thought fucked with Whoodie and causing hell. I was about to go to war behind mine because when it came to my sister, this young ass nigga had me fucked up. I was over letting him have the upper hand because I was considering Keisha's feelings.

"Bet, let's get to it," Ace agreed, as he nodded his head and tucked his gun in the back of his pants.

Walking out of the door, my phone began to ring and I could feel the vibration in my pocket. Usually, I wouldn't even answer calls when I was in this type of mindset but once seeing that it was my grandma calling me, considering the time, I answered it.

"Hello," I answered.

"Jaxsyn… JAXSYN," she screamed into the phone causing my ear to ring. I could hear it in her voice that something was wrong.

"Grandma, what is it?" I asked as I rushed to my car.

"It's Keisha. Omg, it's Keisha." She was crying so hard that she struggled to get her words out. Her voice was shaky and I could hardly understand her.

Whatever it was concerning Keisha had my grandma worked up, but I needed her to calm down. At her age, the last thing I needed was for her to make herself sick which would be something else I had to be stressed about.

"What is it, Grandma?" I tried to remain calm as I hopped in my car and so did Ace.

"She's in the hospital Jaxsyn. Hurry up and get there. Me and Pops are on our way. They say it's bad." My grandma continued to cry as my head began to spin.

The fuck did they mean by it's bad? I pondered as I continued to listen to my grandma cry and sniffle on the phone. Now my head was throbbing and it felt like somebody was squeezing my damn brain. Everything around me was becoming a blur and my only concern was getting to where my sister was, with hopes that it wasn't too bad.

"What hospital Ma?" I asked.

"BenTab," she replied with a shaky voice. I then hung up the phone and began to speed so damn fast. I didn't give a fuck about a cop right now.

"What's the word?" Ace asked me as I continued to stare straight ahead.

"She's in the hospital. That's all I know," I answered dryly. I didn't feel like talking and plus, I didn't know shit.

Finally, I pulled up to the hospital and parked my car front and center. Right now, I didn't care about the rules and regulations. They were just going to have to get over it or serve my ass a ticket.

Rushing out of the car, I barged through the automatic doors as I

6

scanned the waiting room area. To my surprise, I had beat my grandma here.

"Where the fuck is my sister?" I roared once I made my way to the glass window, where a skinny ass white man in a blue scrub sat in a black chair.

"Sir." The security guard, who was wearing his pants a little too tight, walked from behind the podium and headed towards me.

"Step the fuck back before you be laying in one of these hospital rooms," I warned him. It wasn't like he could help me with anything so he was the last person I wanted talking to me.

"Sir, in order for anyone to help you, you will have to calm down." His fat ass, rent a cop looking ass spoke as he held his hands out in front of him, as if that would calm me down.

"I don't need you to tell me shit. Are you the doctor? You got a degree around this bitch? Fuck no, so go back over there to your little corner and eat those donuts you got over there." I mugged him.

Ace then stepped between the two of us because he knew that right now, nobody was safe.

"Nigga, in order for us to see what's up with sis, we first have to get someone to tell us. Shit, I understand you are mad right now, but you have to calm down so these white folks will actually talk to yo' ass right now. You up in here looking like a big ass grizzly bear and shit, these folks two seconds away from calling the cops," Ace said through clenched teeth while looking over his shoulder, observing the two.

He was right though. I was going about this all the wrong way. I needed to calm down if I wanted to get anywhere with these damn people.

Right when I was about to ask them as nicely as I could, in walked my grandma.

"Ahh, my baby," she let out so loudly then broke down, falling to the floor.

Everybody in the waiting room heads were now focused directly on us. I had already caused a scene and now my grandma was causing an even bigger one.

Rushing over to her, I helped lift my grandma up off of the floor and we walked her over to one of the beige leather chairs. Her poor little body was shaking as if it was below zero and her eyes were way puffier than normal. I could tell that she had been crying hard because her eyes were red and sat low.

"I keep telling her she is going to have to calm down before she be right up in the hospital with Keisha. She knows how her blood pressure is." My grandpa wiped his forehead as he looked down at his wife, who was now rocking back and forth in the chair.

I could see the worry lines printed on his forehead. He was just as stressed as my grandma but being the man that he was, he wore a brave face. He knew that one of them had to be the strong one.

"I got her. Just go see what you can find out about your sister." He patted me on the back then sat down next to my grandma. He began to rub her back and allowed her to lay her head on his shoulder.

I swear, them two were the definition of real love because I knew that no matter what, my grandpa was going to be what my grandma needed during whatever situation, and vice versa.

Exhaling, I tried to ignore the continuous headache. I just needed somebody to tell me something, anything.

As I walked back to the window, I counted down from ten then braced myself once I got to the window. The same scrawny white man was looking at me with a beet-red face.

Let me try this again. I sighed and paused while running my hands over my waves then down my face. "I'm here because my grandma was alerted by the Houston Police Department that my sister is here— La'Keisha King," I spoke way calmer than I did the first time with hopes that he would hurry up and start typing on the keyboard.

"Hold on one second," the guy spoke and began tapping on the keyboard as he looked at the screen.

"I see her in our system. If you give me one moment, I will alert the doctor that her family is here." He gave me a faint smile before he picked up the phone and made a call.

Huffing, I nodded my head then turned and walked away. I went and sat down next to my grandma as we continued to wait. She was still on edge as she rocked back and forth. The only good thing was that she was no longer crying hard, but I could still hear her light sniffles which hurt a nigga's soul.

"I told you to go get my baby..." She looked at me as if it was my fault that something happened to Kiesha.

"What did you want me to do?" I looked at her confused.

"You are the big brother. You were supposed to drag her ass out of there. If she was mad, she would have gotten over it, Jaxsyn." My grandma raised her voice. She was upset at me and was trying to place the blame on me when it wasn't my fault. Yeah, I was Keisha's big brother and yeah, I should have dragged her ass out of there, but I wasn't thinking about that at the time. My biggest concern was not having my sister mad at me or pushing away from me but shit, look where that got me.

Sighing, this was one of those times I decided to stay quiet. Never would I ever disrespect my grandma, so it was best that I kept my mouth closed and let her feel however she felt.

As I sat there impatiently waiting for the doctor to come from the back, the door opened and it was like everything went silent as my heart raced. Anger filled my body; my hands shook and the only thing I saw was red. Without even thinking twice about it, I leaped to my feet and pulled my gun. All of the people that were waiting to be seen started screaming and falling to the floor. Some even took a run for it!

In the background, I could hear my grandma and grandpa calling my name but right now, I didn't care. Whoodie had some explaining to do.

"What happened to my fucking sister?" I roared as I slammed him up against the wall and kept the gun pointed at his head.

I wanted to beat his ass right then and there. I wanted to kill him because I was blaming him. It was because of him why I was up at the hospital instead of at home with my little sister, somewhere in her new room, ducked off.

"Fuck yo' sister," he had the nerve to say, and I lost it.

Even though I knew I couldn't openly commit a murder, that wasn't going to stop me from beating his ass.

"Bitch, what?" I scrunched up my face right as I hit him upside the head with my gun. I was raining blow after blow until he finally collapsed on the white tile floor.

His lil' weak ass was no match for me, but that was known. Every time he tried to swing, I ducked and dodged it then connected with his face. It was no competition and before he could even get himself together, he was back falling to the floor.

Blood was coming from everywhere on him and I still wasn't satisfied.

"Jaxsyn stop. You gotta stop," my grandma screamed.

I easily tuned her out and continued releasing all of my frustrations out on him.

"Jaxsyn, you gotta get out of here before the laws come," Ace suggested as he pulled me up off of him.

"Fuck the law!" I said out of breath as I broke free from Ace and continued to whoop Whoodie's ass.

That nigga was weak and today proved it. Shit, the fact that he still hadn't done shit about me killing some of his crew proved it.

"Jaxsyn, your sister. You gotta get out of here." Ace pulled me off of him again.

"Jaxsyn, you don't need to be in jail. You need to be there for your sister." He tried to talk some sense into me, but I wanted to beat Whoodie's ass for my sister and also be there for her.

"Leave Jaxsyn." Ace looked at me and I reluctantly left. I hated that I had to leave before I had heard anything about my sister, but I had to. I didn't want to be in jail and something was severely wrong with Kiesha.

I looked around at the scene then rushed out the doors. I sprinted to my car and got in and as I was leaving, I could hear the sirens getting closer.

Kaizlyn

*I*t had been three days. Three long days since I had heard from Jaxsyn. I didn't know what all was going on besides the stuff that my grandma had told me.

She had informed me that Keisha was hit by a car and wasn't doing too well. She told me that her family didn't know if she was going to make it. That she had internal bleeding on her brain and had to have surgery and that she slipped into a coma after her surgery. I knew that Jaxsyn was probably taking it badly and all I wanted to do was be there for him.

Exhaling, I turned over on my back and stared at the ceiling fan as it went around in circles. I had nothing else to do with my time. I had no phone, no tv, nothing. All the things that a normal teen would be addicted to and doing at my age, I was stuck in the house living a boring life.

As I laid there bored out of my mind, the light taps on my door caused me to sit up.

"Hey baby, you want to go to the store with me?" my grandma smiled and asked.

Since I didn't have anything else to do, I figured that going to the store with her would be the most excitement I would get for a while.

"Yeah I'll go." I climbed out of my bed and put my shoes on. I was still dressed from when I got out of school earlier.

After putting my shoes on, I walked into the living room and my grandma was waiting by the door with her purse.

"Ready?" she asked, and we left out of the house.

As we made our way to the car, my heart dropped when I saw Jaxsyn pull up. I didn't know why, but I stopped my stride as my grandma continued to walk to the car.

"I'm coming Grandma," I let her know.

Nibbling down on my bottom lip, I debated for about five seconds, then bravery took over me as I walked across the grass and up to Jaxsyn's car. With a deep sigh, I knocked on the car window.

"What's up?" He let the window down and looked at me as if he didn't even know me.

"How you been?" I asked.

"Good." He gave me a dry reply which had me wishing I would have never walked over here to talk to him.

I had to admit, Jaxsyn didn't look like his normal self. He looked so stressed and I desperately wanted to help make his day better. I could see it in eyes that he wasn't getting any sleep.

"Well, I was just checking on you since I haven't heard from you," I let him know softly. Hoping that he would pick up off of my vibe and be more welcoming to my presence.

"Well you don't have a phone so what do you want me to do?" he said nastily, and I stepped back, shocked.

"What is your problem?" I questioned him.

"Look Kaizlyn, I'm not in the mood for all these fucking questions." He stepped out of his car and looked down at me.

His harsh way of saying what he said, had hurt my feelings. I couldn't believe that he was being so mean to me when all I was trying to do was check on him. The way he was acting, you would think that we weren't good just a few days ago.

"Really Jaxsyn? Really?" I paused and looked him up and down.

He stood before me without a care in the world. His facial expression was stoic and I wanted so badly for him to soften up and talk to me, but he just shrugged his shoulders and began texting on his phone.

"Fuck you Jaxsyn," I hissed as I stormed away from him.

Like, don't get me wrong, I knew that he was stressed over his sister but still…that was not a valid reason for him to do me this type of way. To be an asshole to me as if he wasn't just asking me to be his girl. As if he wasn't just deep in me, making my body feel amazing.

Ugh, I wanted to scream from frustration and a whole bunch of other emotions. Rushing to my grandma's car, I got in and buried my head into my hands. To say my feelings were hurt would be an understatement.

I was now regretting moving so fast with him. I wished that I would have waited longer to let him have me but I didn't, and now my feelings were involved. There was no undoing any of it and I was now feeling so fucking stupid.

"Everything ok?" my grandma asked before she cranked the car up.

"Yeah, everything is ok," I replied as I sat up and dried my face.

"No, it's not. You've fallen for that damn boy already." She looked at me with sympathetic eyes.

She was right though, I had fallen for Jaxsyn. It was so easy to do. It was like he knew what to say and when to say it. Now I was feeling stupid because I should have known better. But he was so fine and perfect. The way he would sag just a little, the jewelry that he would wear when he dressed up and even when he dressed down in something so simple as a white tee and some basketball shorts, would have me gazing at him. The way he cared for his sister and wanted to protect her. The way he spoke to my body and the way he showed me that he cared enough about me to listen to my painful memories from my past. He made me feel like there could be something between the two of us, but I guess I was wrong. Matter fact, there was no guessing. I was wrong. He didn't care, and he made that obvious by the way that he just acted.

He is such a fucking asshole, I thought to myself as I blew out a flustered breath.

"I did but that is over with now." I crossed my arms and sat back in the seat.

"He could just be hurting Kaizlyn. When people hurt, they shut others out. Sometimes that's the only way people know how to cope with certain things," my grandma stated as she gave me the side-eye.

Sighing, I tucked a piece of hair behind my ear. She was right because I remember when I was dealing with my mother's death and everything else that happened during that time, I shut everyone out. I didn't talk much and I stayed to myself. The only person that I felt comfortable enough to talk to was Emma, and that was because she could relate to how I felt due to the fact that she lost her mom too.

"I'm over it. Forget him." I rolled my eyes because even though I understood what she was saying, I felt like Jaxsyn didn't have to be an asshole about it. Especially after the moments we shared with each in such a short period of time. I wanted to listen to what was causing him pain and try my best to heal it or be there for him. I didn't want him to shut me out.

"Uhm. Huh." My grandma poked her lips out then began driving off.

Not saying anything else about how I felt when it came to Jaxsyn, I put my feelings on the back burner and tried to focus on other things. Like the test I had coming up Friday.

Who am I lying to? I pouted to myself. I wasn't worried about no damn test right now. Jaxsyn had me deep off in my feelings and I was slowly drowning in them.

Pulling up to Kroger, my grandma parked her car in the first handicap parking spot and we both got out and headed inside.

"You ever thought about getting a job?" my grandma questioned as she grabbed the buggy and began to push it down aisle eight.

"Nah, I haven't." I looked around.

No, I had never thought about getting a job. I never had to but now that she said it, it didn't sound like a bad idea.

"Oh, ok. Here, I think you can start at sixteen. I understand if you don't want one but I feel like it will be a big help for you. I know at your age, you young folks be wanting certain stuff." She continued to talk as she threw two packs of cornbread mix into her basket.

"You're right," I agreed.

We continued to talk about the whole job thing as she continued to throw different things in the basket. Once we finally finished, we headed to the counter and before my grandma could even unload her basket, the man that was behind the counter greeted her with the biggest smile.

"Hey Mrs. Daisey," the older guy with salt and pepper hair spoke to my grandma.

Looking at his name tag, I saw that his name was Thomas. Thomas was a taller dude, who was a shade lighter than the night's skin. His skin tone was a smooth, black color but to be his age, he was easy on the eyes.

"Hey, Mr. Thomas." My grandma blushed and smiled from ear to ear.

"What you cooking today? I might need to come by and get a meal," he beamed. His eyes glowed as he stared at my grandma.

I could tell by the way he looked at her, that he enjoyed seeing her in the store and could possibly have a crush on her.

"Just some dressing, mac and cheese and some corn. Just something simple," she replied as she dug into her purse to pull her card out as I stared at them and also took the remainder of the stuff out of the basket.

"Oh my. I need to come over there." He continued to talk and laugh with her.

My grandma had no clue that he was flirting with her and it was so funny to me.

"Hey Thomas, this is my granddaughter. You think you can get her a job up here?" she asked him as I grabbed the groceries that were now bagged up and put them in the basket.

"Grandbaby," he said with surprise. "Faith had a baby?" he asked, and my grandma nodded her head and I saw her take a big gulp.

"Yes, Faith had a baby." She nodded, keeping it short and sweet.

"Oh wow, where is she? I haven't seen her since she was around her age." Mr. Thomas wore a big smile on his face as me and my grandma's faces were painted with sadness.

"Oh, did I say something wrong?" He placed his hand over his heart as he stared at us.

"No, it's just... it's just, I lost her months ago. She was murdered," my grandma stated lowly.

Mr. Thomas gasped and placed his hand over his mouth then said, "Sorry to hear that Daisey. So sorry," he continued as he pressed something on the keyboard so that my grandma could pay for her items.

"Well, if she wants the job, she can come up here Saturday and start," he let my grandma know. He was talking to her about it as if I was not standing there.

"You hear him, baby?" She looked over at me and gave me a faint smile.

"Yes ma'am." I nodded.

"Ok, well thank you, Thomas. I will have her in here Saturday." My grandma smiled. "Around what time?" she added.

"Ten o'clock. I will be here." He smiled and then waved us goodbye as we headed for the exit door.

As me and my grandma headed to our car, the girl who always popped up at Jaxsyn's house was walking up. I could see her little baby bump which reminded me of why I needed to let him go. He was going to be having a baby soon and I knew that wouldn't do anything but get in our way. There was no way that he would pick spending time with me over spending time with his child which also meant spending time with his child's mother. Thinking about all of it was making my head spin.

When she passed by me, she rubbed her belly then smirked at me. I shook my head at her childish antics. I wasn't trying to have beef with her.

"What bitch, don't be shaking your head at me." She turned towards me.

"What's your problem?" I asked her as she began to walk closer to me.

"Hold up now, what is going on?" my grandma questioned. She had stopped putting the groceries in the car and was now headed towards where I stood.

"My problem is that you need to leave my fucking man alone. I don't know why he's acting like he wants you when he has a baby on the way," she snapped.

Never did Jaxsyn willingly bring up his and her relationship. I had honestly put two and two together. I mean, I knew it had to be a reason why she was acting such a fool behind him.

"He is not my man and you don't have to worry about me and him," I let her know.

"Good, don't let me catch you around him either," she spat then walked away.

I felt my grandma's hand on my back, and I flinched. I turned around and looked at her. Her expression was full of empathy.

"Come on baby." She guided me to the car and I followed.

I hated that it was coming to this but with Jaxsyn and his asshole ways plus his baby mama drama, there was no way that we were going to work. I was too young to be dealing with this type of shit, and I wasn't.

Whoodie

*T*wisting my head from side to side as Chyna massaged my back, I sat deep in my thoughts. My body was still sore and my jaw was slowly going down after having Jaxsyn's bitch ass jump on me. I swear on everything I love, I wanted that nigga's head. He had played me for a coward one too many times and I wasn't having it anymore.

"How does this feel baby?" Chyna hummed in my ear as she rubbed my shoulders.

"Good." I picked up the already rolled blunt and grabbed the lighter off of the brown wood, square table.

Lighting the blunt, I took one long puff and held that shit in. I was stressed the fuck out. Jaxsyn had just killed off half of the niggas on my team and one of them was my fucking cousin. Then to make shit worse, Sims was in the hospital after damn near dying. He had lost a lot of blood but thank God I got that nigga to the hospital when I did. When he arrived at the hospital, he was unconscious and they had to give him a lot of blood. I still couldn't believe that nigga made it. If it wasn't for Chyna applying pressure, he probably would have died.

Exhaling, I released the smoke in my mouth as I tried to relax and come up with a plan.

"What you thinking about baby?" Chyna made her way to the front of me.

She was wearing short booty shorts which had her sexy, plump ass on display.

"You putting my dick in your mouth," I replied as I hit the blunt again.

Chyna was fine and stood up like a stallion. I had met her at a gas station and I couldn't let her ass pass me by. She was fine as fuck and way thicker than Keisha. The day I got Chyna's number, her ass let me hit that same night. I later found out that she went to a high school on the other side of town. I referred to it as the uppity side.

I was able to still fuck her and stay with Keisha because we went to two different schools but the more Chyna got the dick, the more she wanted to make herself present. Who was I to tell her no though? She thought that she was my girl just like Keisha did.

"I got you Daddy." She fell down to her knees and unleashed the beast who needed special attention.

"You got me Maw?" I rested my head on the back of the couch as I hit the blunt.

"I got you Daddy." She smiled as she gently stroked my dick.

"Well get to work," I let her know.

Chyna let her tongue glide against her top lip. She swirled some spit around in her mouth as she gripped my dick tightly with her right hand.

Leaning forward, as she held my dick, she let droplets of spit drizzle down on the head of my dick as if she was decorating my dick with caramel, like a banana split.

Slowly using the spit as a lubricant, she stroked my dick making it harder than it already was.

"Make it nasty baby." I reached over and ashed the blunt in the ashtray.

"You know it," she moaned and then deep throated my whole dick.

"Mhmm," she hummed as my dick touched the back of her throat.

She continued to jab at the back of her throat as if she had no tonsils. The longer she kept it at the back of her throat, the wetter her mouth got.

"Yeah baby, like that. Shit," I hissed.

Hitting the blunt again, I swear the best thing in the world was getting head and smoking a blunt. I was so fucking relaxed that I could feel tingling in my damn toes.

Gargling on my dick and massaging my balls, Chyna popped my dick out of her mouth and when she did, drool followed.

"Mhmm, I love the way yo' dick taste. Fuck," she moaned. "It makes me so fucking wet," she hissed between her teeth.

Chyna then pulled her shorts to the side and dipped two fingers into her center. "Ahhh," she moaned out as her head fell back and she played with her clit.

That shit was so fucking sexy and my dick was now rock fucking hard. That shit was sexy watching her play with her pussy.

Chyna took her fingers out of her pussy and smeared all of her juices onto my dick and went back to sucking it.

"I taste so good," she let out.

"Let me taste," I told her, and she stopped sucking and dipped her fingers back into her pussy and when she pulled her fingers out, they were coated in her nectar.

I grabbed her hand and brought her fingers up to my nose first, inhaling her scent. Once I saw that she smelled good, I stuck her fingers in my mouth and licked off all of her sweetness.

"Now finish, so I can nut," I told her, and she forcefully shoved my dick back down her throat.

This time, she didn't stop. She didn't slow down. She was bobbing on my dick and choking so damn hard that tears were coming out of her eyes.

"Shit." I hit the blunt again. "Damn," I exhaled.

Looking down as Chyna did that lil' thing I liked with her tongue around the head of my dick, my nut was now right at the tip of my dick.

"Suck that mothafucka," I told her, and she began sucking on it as if it was a popsicle.

"I want to nut on your face." I stopped her and stood to my feet.

I then released all of my seeds on her face, painting a pretty picture.

"Fuck," I howled as the blunt began to burn down and burn my damn finger.

"Shit." I dropped it and it went right down Chyna's shirt.

"Ahh," she screamed. "Shit." She hopped up and began to shake her shirt until the dubbie fell out and hit the ground.

She was looking like a damn fool with nut all over her face as she jumped up and down while trying not to get burned.

"Ughh Whoodie, fuck," she said with aggravation.

"What? Fuck." I looked at her. She was doing too much because it wasn't that damn serious.

"Go get me a damn towel so I can clean my face," she demanded, but I stuffed my dick back in my pants and sat back down.

I needed to handle some other shit right now. I needed to see what had been heard at the spot that I knew Jaxsyn and his team hung out at.

"Fuck you. Ugh," she complained as she stormed off towards the bathroom.

While she was gone to wipe my kids off of her face, I picked up my phone and text my homie, Dex. I had been having him go and chill at the lil' spot. He would either get a cut, throw some dice, or pretend to be getting along with those weak ass niggas that be up there. Dex was an older cat and he was with the shits. Always ready to get down and dirty if need be.

He had been texting me everything that he heard which was not much, but it was enough. It was enough for me to know that Jaxsyn was in his feelings about his sister which meant his focus was off.

I wanted to make a move on Jaxsyn soon because I knew his mind wasn't right due to the fact that his precious baby sister was sitting in ICU right now. It was kind of funny because I was never really going to kill her. I was just going to drive that nigga Jaxsyn crazy making threats and shit. I knew he would weaken due to the fact that I had his sister. And that shit would have worked had Keisha not escaped. Which got me to thinking. It never really made sense to me on how she even got out.

"So how did Keisha escape again?" I asked Chyna once she walked back into the room with a clean face.

For a moment, she stood there with a dumbfounded look upon her face and then she began to talk. "Uhmm. Uhmm. She broke loose. I had walked in to tell her to stop screaming and somehow she broke loose."

She was explaining it to me, but I didn't believe her. She couldn't even make eye contact with me. The whole time she was talking to me, she stared off looking at everything but me. I had a feeling that it was more to the story than that.

Getting up, I threw my dreads out of my face as I walked towards her. I grabbed her by the cheeks so that she could look me directly in my eyes and attempt to tell me that same lie she had just let ease off her lips so easily.

"Are you lying to me, Chyna?" I calmly asked.

I could see her body trembling slightly as I stood there waiting for her to speak.

"Hello," I mouthed as she darted her eyes from being locked with mine to the floor.

"Nah, I'm up here baby girl." I placed my finger underneath her chin and lifted her head up. "Tell me Chyna."

"I told you that she got lose. I don't know how. I went in there because she was screaming." Chyna was fidgety as she talked to me which led me to think she was lying.

"What did her screaming have to do with you though?" I questioned her because she had no business going in there, but Chyna just had to make her presence known.

I knew how bitches worked. She wanted to rub some shit in Keisha's face while she was at her lowest.

"So where were you when she stabbed Sims?" I questioned.

"I told you that she…she…she head-butted me," she stuttered.

"Chyna, stop fucking lying to me man." I hemmed her up and backed her up against the wall.

She was lying to me in my fucking face and I didn't like that shit.

"I'm not lying to you. I swear." Her voice was shaky and her eyes were glossy.

"You better not be lying to me. I have a feeling that you are and you better hope Sims don't tell me otherwise, whenever he's able to talk," I let her know, and she quickly nodded her head.

"Get on." I shoved her and she dropped to the ground being all dramatic and shit.

Chyna was such a cry baby. She would talk her shit but couldn't really back it up without tears falling. I swear, that shit wrecked my nerve. The night at the party when I told her to go home, she cried. She cried and acted a fool. I literally had to fuck her real quick in her car just so that she would dry her fucking eyes and leave. I also had to promise her that I would come to her house and sneak in through the window, but I never did.

Which was why I had to leave Keisha at the house that morning and go to Chyna's house just so that she could stop blowing up my phone.

No lie, when I got back, I wasn't expecting to see Sims fucking my bitch, even though I did fuck up a lot. That shit, that was a down bad. It caught me by surprise and it stung a little.

I was one of those niggas that wanted to do what the fuck I wanted to do but any bitch I was fucking couldn't. That was law.

"It's time for you to go." I looked over my shoulder at her.

"What?" She looked up at me with red eyes.

"Get yo' ass up and go home. Did I stutter?" I hissed.

"Fuck you Whoodie," she spat.

Everything in me wanted to turn around and let her know who she was fucking with, but I needed to get all my ducks in a row so that I could take down this nigga Jaxsyn and take over. But also get revenge for all of the hell he was currently causing in my life.

Chyna stormed over to the table and picked up her keys and her phone. She then turned and looked at me with a puppy dog pout and tears still in her eyes.

"Bye," I yelled, and she scurried out of the house, slamming the fucking door behind her.

Sitting back down on the couch, I looked over at the stain of blood that now decorated the carpet. I had already tried to steam clean it and yet it was still visible. I knew that I was going to have to figure something out before my people got back in town and saw that shit on their floor. They had gone back to Louisiana for two months, leaving me all alone in the house. Shit, I even had to figure out how I was going to fix the hole in the wall that I had just noticed.

Huffing, I scratched the side of my head as I pondered on what else I could do to remove the stain. My ass needed it gone because when my auntie came back, I didn't want to have to explain anything. She for sure didn't play that shit and if she felt like there was a sense of drama on her front step, she was acting a fool.

"Fuck," I cursed as I shook my head. Picking up the cigar, I bust it down the middle and walked to the kitchen to empty the center of it in the trash. I then rolled me up a fat ass blunt and smoked all my pain and stress away.

Chyna

*W*iping my damn tears away, I got in the car and sped off. I didn't even know why I had got caught up with Whoodie in the first place. All he did was feed me lies and I would fall for the shit. I even called myself cheating on Melo for him. God knows if Melo knew that I was seeing someone else he would have a fit, but when I saw Whoodie's fine ass I couldn't turn him down.

He just screamed thuggish, with a pocket full of money, and not to mention the night I saw him at the gas station he was dressed down to the T and his accent caused me to want to know more about him. I was curious.

Any other time, I would have had my nose in the air because niggas tried to talk to me all the time. I knew it was because of the fact at the age of seventeen, I was built like a grown ass woman. My body was banging. I knew that I had a big ass and big breasts which had been getting me a lot of attention since I was in the ninth grade.

As I drove back to my side of town, my phone began to ring. I had been ignoring Melo a lot lately. I had even been missing school since all that shit happened with Sims being stabbed. If it hadn't been for me, he probably would have died.

At first, when I heard the sirens I thought that they were coming for Sims, but I had to remember I didn't call them. That also left me to wonder did Keisha call them but when Whoodie burst through the house, with a panicked expression, asking me what happened, I was too in shock to answer and plus, we had to act fast and get Sims to the hospital.

So Whoodie pulled his car in the garage and we eased Sims into the car. I was so scared that he was going to die. He had lost so much blood and I heard that getting stabbed in the neck was deadly and deep down, I just didn't think that he would make it.

Whoodie had ordered for me to change clothes, bag my shit up and leave his house thirty minutes after he did. I did exactly what he told me, ignoring all of the chaos that was going on outside.

Sighing, I shook those thoughts away the moment my phone went to ringing again. I looked down, saw it was Melo and reluctantly answered the phone. "Yes."

"Why the fuck haven't you been answering your phone? Where have you been? Yo' people have been calling me asking about you." His voice escalated as he asked question after question.

"I've been laying low that is all." I sighed into the phone.

"Man, Chyna baby, fuck," Mello exhaled into the phone and I rolled my eyes.

I wasn't even in the mood to talk to him. Whoodie had me in a bad mood and I just wanted to go home and lay down. I knew that when I got home my mom would have a lot to say, but I was hoping she wasn't there. I was hoping just like always she was gone somewhere with one of her many men that she dated.

"What Mello?" I said with annoyance.

"I really need to talk to you. I got something to tell you." He sounded so distressed and worried, which wasn't like him.

"What do you want to talk about? What is it?"

"We can't talk about it over the phone. Meet me in our spot," he said into the phone.

I couldn't go meet him though, not yet. I needed to go home, take a bath and brush my teeth. I didn't want to go in front of Melo smelling like a whole other nigga's dick.

"Let me go home first. You know my mom is probably losing it."

"Ok, hit me up when you ready," he let me know, and I just hung up the phone.

After ending the call, I scrolled through my call log and stared at Whoodie's name in my phone. I was currently debating on if I wanted to call him and talk about what had just happened.

Ugh, I expressed as I locked my phone, threw it over in the passengers' seat and banged on the steering wheel. Whoodie was a nigga I should have just left alone. I was hooked to his thug ass and that bomb ass dick he had.

Pulling up into my yard, I saw that my mother was home. I was pretty sure she didn't even care about me not being home, and the only reason she was calling looking for me was because the school was calling her.

Once I shut my car off, I got out and headed inside. The first thing I heard was the radio blasting and my mother was in the middle of the living room dancing in her workout clothes. She was really big on staying fit and fine. She had a thin waist and big booty. She acted young and still ran the streets as if she was a teenager.

"Chyna," out of breath, she called my name as she turned down the stereo with the remote.

"What Mom?" I signed.

"Why haven't you been to school, Chyna? If I have to pay any fees or go to jail because of you, it's your ass." She tried to sound serious but I could tell she didn't even care.

"Ok, Mom. I'll be going to school tomorrow," I stated as I stormed up the stairs. I could still hear her talking as I made my way up.

Once reaching my room, I immediately stripped out of my clothes and headed into my bathroom. I cut the shower on then once it was hot I got in. Rinsing away all of my deceitful shit, I got out and wrapped the towel around me. With the towel still around my body, I brushed my teeth and combed through my extensions.

Now refreshed, I slipped on a pair of PINK white and green tights and a shirt that matched. I slipped, on my PINK slides and grabbed my phone so that I could call Melo and see if he still wanted to meet up. Even though I wanted to rest, there was no point because eventually, he would call again, so I needed to get it over with now.

"Hey, you still want to meet up?" I asked him the moment he answered the phone.

"Yeah, are you leaving your house right now?" he questioned me, and I stood up, walked over to my dresser and sprayed my body down with Red from Bath and Body Works.

"Yes." I grabbed my keys and headed out of my room door.

"Ok. See you there." He paused. "Hey Chyna, I love you."

"I love you too Melo," I dryly replied as I walked down the stairs.

"Call you when I'm there." I hung up the phone because I knew that I was about to have to answer more questions from a woman that didn't even much care about me, but it was cool. If she wanted to play the mother figure this week then I would just play along with her.

"Where do you think you're going?" she asked me.

She was now sitting down on the sofa, cleaning from underneath her nails with a metal nail file.

"I'll be right back. I'm going to meet Melo," I let her know, and she smiled.

Of course she did, because she loved Melo. She liked him so much that she would let him come over and stay as long as he wanted to, which was crazy. She would wear really tight clothes, which annoyed me because I felt like she should cover up and show some type of respect and actually look like my mother instead of one of my friends.

"Oh, Melo." She added emphasis when she said his name. "Ok, baby. Tell him hey and to come over for dinner sometime." She winked and I rolled my eyes and headed out of the door.

As I was headed to my car, the sky was starting to rumble and I could smell the scent of rain in the air. Getting into my car that my mom had got me a few months back, I stuck my key in the ignition and headed to me and Melo's spot.

It wasn't like a secret spot, it was just one where we would sit on the roof of his or my car and just talk. Even though sex was a major factor when we first got together, we ended up finding other things that we actually liked doing. I used to love sitting on the hood of the car and just talking about shit. But ever since I met Whoodie, Melo had been on the back burner.

After driving about fifteen minutes out, I drove down this dirt road and parked my car next to Melo's. He was already sitting on the hood of his Mustang, staring off into the beautiful trees that surrounded us.

"Hey," I spoke as I tugged on the sleeve of my hoodie and went and had a seat beside him.

"Hey, I missed you," he confessed as he turned and pulled me in for a hug.

"Miss you too," I lied. I hadn't missed him. I had my mind on so many other things with the drama Whoodie had going on, I had no time to miss him. I hadn't even been thinking about him.

Pulling back from him, I was now straddling between his legs. He had his hands resting on my ass and he was just staring at me.

"What is it?" I asked him because he didn't say nothing. He just kept looking at me as if he knew something I didn't know.

"Man," he exhaled as he ran his right hand down his face and then rubbed both of them on his jeans.

"What is it Melo?" I huffed.

"It's a lot of shit Chyna." He paused, cleared his throat and then continued. "So, I know you've been cheating on a nigga or whatever," he confessed, and when he spoke those words my heart fell out of my ass and I began to feel queasy.

"What are you talking about Melo? No, I am not," I lied right in his face. I mean, I wasn't about to confess and plead guilty to some shit if he didn't have valid evidence.

"Yes, you have. Just cut the shit."

"How do you know that?" I stepped away from him.

"Because I've been following you," he admitted, and I was now in full shock.

I wanted to be mad. I wanted to act a big ass fool because I knew that it would then buy me time or give me a reason to just walk off and not have to admit to him that I was cheating.

"Why the fuck are you following me, Melo? That shit is weird." I curled my top lip up as I placed my hands on my hip.

"I wouldn't have to if you weren't out doing foul shit." He jumped off of the hood of his car and began to pace back and forth.

As he continued to walk, he looked up at the sky before he released a big sigh as he continued to rub his hands together. He was in deep thought which made me wonder what else did he know and how long had he been following me.

"But that's beside the point." He paused, turned towards me and the look in his eyes was sadness, fear, and regret. He looked like it was something much heavier than me cheating weighing heavy on him.

"I hit somebody," he stated. With me not thinking much into it, I shrugged my shoulders.

"Ok, and your car doesn't look damaged. So why are you trippin' over a wreck if your car is not messed up?" I questioned, spinning around on my heels and observing his car.

There were no scrapes, paint chipped off, bumper out of place or none of that.

"No, I hit a person. A girl," he confessed as he broke down to the ground.

"I could lose everything. My scholarship for football. I could go to jail." He was now crying like somebody in his family had died.

"Well Melo, did you call the cops?"

"No, I didn't. I took off in my car. I don't even know who the person was I hit. I had been following you and I was in this neighborhood that I had been seeing your car in for the last few days. I was driving through there when my phone was ringing and when I tried to answer, it slipped out of my hand and fell onto the floor. I was reaching down thinking that I was good. When I looked back up, it was too late. I couldn't do anything. I froze." He shook his head as I listened to everything that he had just said.

Wow, I thought. I couldn't believe that it was Melo who had hit Keisha and fled the scene. I was in such disbelief. I knew that if Keisha's brother found out that it would be over for Melo.

"Melo, it's ok. Just continue to act normal. The moment you start acting different, then you look guilty," I tried to coach him.

Even though my head was up Whoodie's ass, I didn't want to see anything bad happen to Melo. Hell, and to be real, Keisha damn near deserved that shit after what she did to me. I still couldn't believe she head-butted me.

"It's killing me though. I don't know. Maybe I need to go to the police." He rose to his feet and began to nervously walk in circles.

"No, calm down. Everything will be ok. They don't know who did it. So just be cool." I walked over to him and he wrapped his arms around me tightly.

"Thank you, Chyna," he whispered in my ear.

"For what?" I asked him.

"Just for being there and understanding," he replied before he kissed me on the lips.

We stood there, arms wrapped around each other as our tongues slithered and danced in each other's mouths. Crazily, this moment felt right because Melo was so sensitive and soft compared to Whoodie who was, rough and rude.

Feeling raindrops begin to fall down on my head, I screamed as I took off running to my car. I wasn't trying to get my hair wet.

Before I pulled off, Melo ran up to the window and I rolled it down.

"Thank you again, and if you want to be just friends, it's cool with me," he stated.

"Yeah, it might be what's best," I agreed, and he bobbed his head.

"Alright. It's cool. Catch you around and Chyna, please don't tell no one." He side-eyed me and I brought my fingers up and crossed them, making a promise to him that I wouldn't tell nobody.

"Aite." He then tapped the hood of my car and walked over to his car.

Sighing, I put my car in reverse and headed home.

Melo

Boom!

*J*umping up out of my sleep, there were beads of sweat on my forehead and my whole body was soaking wet. Ever since I hit ol' girl, I had been having a hard time going to sleep and when I did finally go to sleep, the dreams would come back and haunt me. Reminding me of what I did.

Fuck, I thought as I closed my eyes tight and ran my hands down my face. Sitting up in the bed, I threw the covers off of me and sat up.

I kept telling myself that all this shit would blow over, but I was so on the edge that I was about to make myself go to the cops just so that I could tell them what happened.

After I hit the girl, I sped off and used a pay phone to make the call to 911. I had remembered the street and directed them to where she was. Once the phone call was made, I sped off. The first thing I did was go to an auto shop so that they could fix my car. It wasn't really damaged, but my right headlight was cracked. I had used some of the money that I had saved up from the part-time job that I had. They quickly fixed it and I had been laying low ever since. I wasn't driving all over town like I normally would. Instead, I would go to school, work, and come home. I hated that I was even in the neighborhood that I was in. Had it not been for me trying to follow Chyna, I would have never been in this situation.

"Shit," I exhaled. I fucked up and let my feelings for Chyna have me running around here on some sucka shit when I should have known better. She was quick and easy. So quick and easy that I had left Kaizlyn for her.

"Kaizlyn," I repeated her name one more time because it had been a minute since I thought about her.

Karma had truly paid me a visit because me leaving her for Chyna was a big mistake. Hurting her the way that I had was fucked up, and now I'm paying for the shit.

Getting out of the bed, I went to the bathroom and took a piss. *Ahh.* I relaxed as I drained my dick then washed my hands and dried them off. I walked out of the bathroom while looking down at my Apple watch. It was three in the morning and I had school in a few hours. Sleep was the last thing on my mind right now but I still got back in the bed, laid down and looked up at the ceiling. I was wondering where I went wrong and how I could get my life back on track.

Beep! Beep! Beep!

My alarm had gone off, making me pop up as if the laws were banging on the door to come get me.

Damn. I reached over and hit the big, round button to silence the noise. I didn't even realize I had gone back to sleep. The last thing I remembered was lying in bed thinking about my life.

I crept out of bed, washed my face, brushed my teeth, and I also brushed over my waves. Not even in the mood, I wore a pair of black joggers and my black Nike jacket. I placed a pair of my Nike slides on my feet and grabbed up my gym bag and backpack and headed out of my room.

"Hey son, are you good?" my mom asked as I walked into the kitchen and she kissed me on the forehead.

"Yeah, I'm ok," I replied, picking up a piece of toast and stuffing it in my mouth.

"Ok, I was just making sure. You seem a little off lately," she stated as she began rinsing the dishes off and sticking them in the dishwasher.

"I'm good Mom. See you when I get in from school. I don't have to work today," I let her know as I opened the fridge and grabbed a bottle of water.

"Alright son. Love you." She smiled as I began to walk towards the door.

"Love you too," I replied.

I was now out of the house and walking to my car. It was still a little dark with the sun slowly making itself known.

Getting inside, I threw my bags to the back of the car, started my car then connected my phone to the Bluetooth.

As I backed out of the driveway, I turned the volume up as Yella Breezy blasted through my speakers.

Cool, calm and relax, I bobbed my head to the beat and made sure to drive the speed limit as I headed to school. I no longer had to pick Chyna up because ever since she got her new car, she'd been doing her own thing.

Approaching a stop sign, I looked in my rear-view mirror and my heart dropped. Behind me was a cop and even though he had no reason to pull me over, I was nervous. There were a million things going on in my head. For instance, that somebody saw me that day and had reported my car to the cops.

Just put your signal on and turn right, I coached myself as I flicked my signal up and turned right.

Stay calm. I gripped the steering wheel, letting my hands twist backwards and forward as precipitation began to make it hard to grip it.

Red, white and blue lights began to flash and I could literally hear my heart beating in my chest.

They know. Panic began to slither through my body as I continued to drive.

In my mind, I was telling myself to just run. Fuck it!

Don't do that shit. I shook my head. I knew if I kept driving, ain't no telling what would happen. Especially with the way the police moved these days.

Finally, I slowed down and stopped on the side of the road. Looking into the side mirror, I watched the slenderly built cop step out of his car, adjust his pants and head towards me.

I kept my hands on the sterling wheel so that he could see them. I didn't need any reason for them to have a "reason" as to why they killed me.

Hearing light taps on my window, I kept my right hand on the steering wheel and used my left to let the window down.

"Hi sir," I spoke.

"Was you not going to stop?" He examined me as he scanned the inside of my car.

"Oh, yes sir," I answered as a huge lump slid down my throat, making me feel like I couldn't breathe.

"I couldn't tell. Where are you headed to?" he asked me, and I could feel the beads of sweat dripping down my face.

"School," I honestly replied.

"Are you ok? Why are you sweating like that?" he questioned as I quickly wiped my face with the end of my shirt.

"Yes sir, just trying to get to school," I explained.

"Oh ok. Can I see your license and insurance card?" he asked as he eyed me up and down.

"Ughh... Ughh. Yeah," I stuttered over my words as I reached over and grabbed what he asked for out of the glove compartment.

After getting my insurance card and grabbing my driver license out of my wallet, I handed it over.

"Can you get out the car for me please?" He looked at my information as he stepped back.

I could feel the disappointment my mother would feel once she found out what I had done. I began to wish that I was the one who had told her first instead of me having to call her from jail.

Standing outside of the car, I watched the officer walk to his car and I assumed he was typing in my information to run me through his system.

Shit. I sighed as I nervously debated on what I should do. Everything in me said to make a run for it. I knew that if I took off now, with my speed I would be able to lose his ass, but then that meant I would be on the run forever.

Impatiently, I stood against my car waiting for him to come back and tell me that I was under arrest. Finally, after what felt like forever, he came back with my information in his left hand and his right hand on his gun.

"Next time, don't act so nervous. You are free to go, and get that back light fixed. Your blinker isn't working," he let me know, as he handed me back my information.

I wanted to fall to the fucking ground because a nigga thought that he was about to be headed down to central booking. I quickly stuffed my insurance card and my driver license in my back pocket.

"Ok sir, I sure will," I let him know and I turned to walk back to my car.

"And Mr. Melo," he called my name and I stopped. I didn't look back, I just stood frozen.

"Have a good day at school," he stated, and I exhaled.

"Thank you, sir," I replied as I looked over my shoulder.

I then got in my car, buckled my seat belt and headed to school. I was definitely going to get that damn light fixed as soon as I left school. I also needed to get this burden off of my chest.

* * *

Now that school was over, I was rushing out of the doors, trying to get to my car. With my phone up to my ear, I was calling to check on Chyna to see what excuse she had this time. Even though we had agreed to be friends, that didn't mean I didn't still care about her ass. She was slowly losing herself and behind a nigga that probably didn't have shit going for himself.

"Hello," she hummed in the phone.

"Why wasn't you at school Chyna?" I asked her.

"I was too tired." She yawned loudly into the phone causing me to take it down away from my ear.

"Seriously Chyna? Yo' ass ain't gon' graduate but alright, bye," I told her before I hung up the phone in her face. Chyna was blowing me being dumb as fuck.

Reaching my car, I got in and drove to the nearest auto shop, so that I could see what all I needed to do in order to get my damn light fixed.

After getting my back blinker fixed, I had tried to call Chyna again but she didn't answer.

My mind was saying go home, but I also wanted to talk to Chyna or maybe get some pussy from her.

Pulling up to her house, I saw that her mother's car was there and so was Chyna's. I knew Chyna's mama didn't have an issue with me, so I parked my car and went and knocked on the front door.

"Hey, is Chyna here?" I asked when her mother, who may I add was fine as fuck for her age, answered the door.

"Nah baby, she left this morning on her way to school. Said she was getting picked up by you," her mother stated as she leaned up against the railing of the door.

She had her arms crossed underneath her breasts, causing them to sit up higher and pour out of the tight-fitting yellow shirt she had on.

"Ugh, ok," I replied. I didn't know what to say. She wasn't with me at no point today and I didn't want to be the one to rat her out.

"I'm guessing she wasn't with you. Which means her hot ass didn't go to school. Come on in baby while I call her," her mother welcomed me in as she twisted farther into the house.

Following behind her, I went and sat down on their all-white sofa.

"Want something to drink?" she asked, as she picked her phone up and began to dial Chyna's number.

"No ma'am." I rubbed my sweaty palms down my joggers and she smiled, nodded and twisted away.

Even though I knew it was wrong, I was staring at her ass that was sitting up just right in the white and grey tights she had on.

Chyna's mom was very fit. Every time I came over when she was here, she would be working out.

"Baby, she is out being fast. She is getting grounded when she comes back." Her mother huffed then came and sat down right beside me.

Her sweet, yet sweaty scent slithered up my nose and made my dick thump.

The fuck are you doing? I thought to myself as I tried to think of something other than my ex-girlfriend's hot ass mom.

"Well, let me go." I stood to my feet and she did the same.

"Ok baby." She reached over and hugged me really tightly.

Not the church hug, but a hug so tight that my dick was surely pressed up against her.

Pulling away, she looked at me, smirked then grabbed it.

I jumped and backed away. "What you doing?"

"Let me handle that for you." She eyed my dick down and all that did was make it brick up even more.

I stood frozen as she walked closer to me, wrapped her arms around my neck and began to kiss me. She kissed me as if she had been wanting to do this.

Don't do this Melo, I thought to myself, but it was no point. Ms. Jade had dropped down to her knees, pulled my dick out and shoved it in her mouth.

"Shit," I hissed as my heart raced, toes curled and head spun.

She was sucking the fuck out my dick. I mean, better than her damn daughter. I damn sure wasn't leaving until I busted a nut.

Even though this shit was wrong, it felt right for the time being. I mean, it felt good to be relaxed and not stressed. But I knew I would regret it as soon as I busted a nut.

Kaizlyn

*S*aturday was here and I was so dreading the idea of having to work, but I knew that the extra money would be a good thing for me.

Climbing out of the bed, I sighed, ran my fingers through my now loose hair and headed to the bathroom so that I could pee then get ready for whatever today brought.

After peeing I was now brushing my teeth. I washed my face next then headed back into my room so that I could get dressed. Deciding on a pair of black pants, a white shirt and my white Nike's, I was now ready for my first day of work.

Walking out of my room, I entered the living room and my grandma was sitting down looking at a note. A note that had her face distraught.

"What is that?" I asked as I went into the kitchen to fix me a cup of orange juice.

Entering back into the living room, my grandma had now folded the paper up and was twirling it in her hands.

"I don't want to talk about it right now," she let me know as she stood to her feet and left out the living room.

Whatever it was worrying my grandma, I wished that she would open up to me and tell me. Which brought me to think about that guy that had come over. She had yet to let me know who he was and what was it that he was talking about.

"You ready?" She came from around the corner with a fake smile on her face, her purse on her shoulder and her long, pretty hair in a ponytail.

"Yeah," I replied. I then gulped down the rest of the orange juice and took the cup back into the kitchen to place in the sink.

As I walked out behind my grandma, she stopped, locked the door and we proceeded to the car.

The moment I got outside, my heart began to race because Jaxsyn's car was parked next door. He wasn't outside or anything, but just the thought of him being next door was putting me in my feelings. I missed him. I missed him way more than I should.

Sighing, I continued walking to the car. As we drove to the store that I was about to start working at, my mind was racing. If I wasn't thinking about Jaxsyn, I was thinking about what secrets my grandma was trying to hold from me.

"Grandma, who was that man?"

"What man baby?" she turned her music down low and said.

"The one you gave that money to," I replied.

"Oh, that man." She paused and looked straight ahead.

"He is a man that you need to stay away from. If you ever encounter him baby, run in the opposite direction. Please." Her eyes lowered.

"Is that all you're going to tell me?"

"That is all I'm going to tell you right now," she simply said and turned her music back up.

She began humming to a church song and tapping her finger against the steering wheel and rocking from side to side as if she wasn't bothered about it anymore.

Pulling up to Kroger, my grandma put her car in park and looked at me.

"You ready for your first day?" she beamed.

"No," I truthfully answered.

"Well, get ready. You are going to be happy you did it." She smiled as she grabbed her purse from the back of the car.

She began to look through her purse until she pulled out her wallet. She opened her wallet and pulled out both my ID and my social security card. I had totally forgotten about both. When I got to the group home, they had taken it all from me in order to keep up with it.

"You'll need this. Do you need me to go in there with you?" she asked me as she handed both of them over to me.

"No, I think I got it," I told her. I then gave her a big hug and got out of the car.

Walking into the store, Mr. Thomas was standing to the side to greet me. He had papers in his hand and was dressed in some tan slacks and a blue collared shirt. He was smiling really big, so I waved and smiled back.

"Hello, are you ready to fill out your paperwork and start your training?" he asked, and I nodded my head.

"Here you go, we can go in my office where you can have a seat and fill everything out," he informed me.

Following behind him, he pushed the white door open and we entered his office, taking a seat in the fold-out chair. I grabbed a pen off his desk and began to fill out all of the information.

"I will be back in like thirty minutes. Take your time." He smiled and then left out of the office.

As I went over the paperwork, all of the questions were giving me a headache.

Taking a deep breath, I closed my eyes and got myself together. I checked off my availability first then went back to the top and finished filling it out. I didn't put a number down because for one, I didn't know my grandma's cell or house number and for two, I didn't personally have one.

I was now done. I stacked the papers up neatly and was waiting for Mr. Thomas to enter.

"Are you done?" He peeked his head inside.

"Yes sir."

"Good." He walked farther in, picked the papers up and flicked through them.

"Let me show you around the store and then you'll come back and sit at the computer for a few hours. We normally do a drug test but I'm going to pass this time." He winked.

He placed the papers in a manila folder and headed for the door. Mr. Thomas polity showed me around for about fifteen minutes. He then sat me down at the computer to begin orientation.

Whew, I exhaled. I was happy to be getting a break. I was currently headed out of Kroger. I didn't have any money to buy anything but I just wanted to get out of there.

Looking around, there was a pizza joint a little ways down. I decided that I would go sit in there until it was time for me to return from break.

Entering the pizza place which was called MOB pizza, I found me a seat in the corner and sat down.

It smelled amazing in here and my stomach was starting to growl. I was thankful that there were people talking and interacting so they couldn't hear it.

Getting up, I walked to the back where the restroom was and entered. I was hoping that the smell would have disappeared or something, but the smell of pizza lingered throughout the whole building. I was trying to forget the growling of my stomach but standing in here wasn't helping anything either.

Ugh, I sighed as I rushed back out. I had to get the hell out of this place because the way my stomach was cutting up, I knew the smell was only going to bring on hunger pains.

Rushing back to the front of the building, I came to a complete halt. *What in the hell is he doing here?* I pondered. I began to nervously run my hands through my hair while wondering how I looked. I pulled at my shirt then ran my hands over the front of my hair, fixing any wild strands.

Just walk past him like you don't even know him, I thought. I took in one deep breath and began walking. I didn't know why, but I felt like if I held my breath, that would also help me to be invisible to him.

1, 2, 3, 4, 5, 6, 7, … I was counting the steps in my head with each one I took. I was now standing right behind him and he had yet to notice me.

With my head down, I eased right past him. Well, at least I thought I did.

"Hey, can we talk?" He grabbed my arm causing me to look up at him and stop walking.

"Talk about what Jaxsyn? How you were being an asshole to me for no reason?" I sighed as I crossed my arms in front of me.

"I'm sorry about that. I was just in a bad a mood with all the shit going on with my sister," he expressed as the short, chubby black girl with long box braids came and handed him his pizza.

The smell of it caused my stomach to growl so loudly that I knew he heard it. I was so embarrassed as I rested my hand on my stomach, hoping that it would shut the fuck up until I got off in the next three hours. I still had thirty more minutes on my lunch break and I didn't want to spend it getting tortured by Jaxsyn or the smell of his pizza.

"Let's talk over pizza. From the sounds of it, you're hungry." He flashed me a dazzling smile that caused my heart to race, my pussy to tighten and the feelings that I had been feeling for him to tingle throughout my body.

"I guess Jaxsyn. I have to get back to work in thirty minutes tho'," I told him, as I looked down at the cute pink and black watch that my grandma had given me the other day.

"Word...you got a job?" He covered his mouth with his fist as he carried the pizza with his free hand to the same table that I was originally sitting at.

"Yes, I had to. Everybody don't have money like you," I sassed as I sat down across from him.

"It wasn't always like this for me though. I had to hustle for this shit baby." He smirked as he opened the box of pizza and my mouth watered.

Not only for the pizza, but for him too. The way he sat across from me, with a plain white tee on, his three chains around his neck that all had different objects hanging from them, his smooth, chocolate skin, and his deep waves that I knew he brushed at least twenty times a day.

"Dive in," he announced, and I moved way faster than I wanted to but I had to hush my growling stomach.

Stuffing the slice of pizza into my mouth, the hot, cheesy, pepperoni pizza danced and made love to my taste buds.

"So are you going to accept my apology? I've missed you," he asked me as he stuffed his mouth with pizza, gobbling the whole thing in just three bites.

"Why should I?" I asked.

"Because you have no reason why you shouldn't. I ain't did shit to you really."

"Ha. That's why you think. But I have numerous reasons why I shouldn't be fucking with you." I paused. I placed the crust of my pizza down and continued. "For one, you can't pick and choose when you want to be an asshole to me. Also, I don't know because I don't have time for no baby mama drama." I rolled my eyes as I thought about that bitch when she approached me.

"What?" he asked, damn near choking on the food that was in his mouth.

"You heard me. Which part you need me to repeat?" I questioned.

"What you mean baby mama? I don't have a baby mama." He grabbed a napkin and wiped his greasy lips.

"Yeah ok. You don't have to lie to me. I ain't your girl so how can I trip."

"I don't have to lie to nobody. Shit, I don't. I keep shit real. Is that baby mine? Hell nah. Is that what she is saying? Yes. Do I give a fuck, no. Now stop playing with me." Jaxsyn gave me this stern look as he licked his lips and I desperately wanted them all over my body.

"Whatever Jaxsyn. I got to get back to work." I stood to my feet and he grabbed my hand and checked his Apple watch.

"Sit yo' ass down Kaizlyn. You got ten more minutes and I want every last minute. Down to the very second. Mr. Thomas will understand." He winked and I looked at him crazily.

"How you know Mr. Thomas?" I questioned.

"Because I know everybody." He winked at me again and I almost fainted.

Why did this man have to be so damn sexy to me? What was so crazy about it, he knew he was. However, I didn't want to sit here and fall for his every word and then have my heart broken. He already crushed it the other morning when I tried to talk to him.

"So how is your sister?" I asked as I sat back down.

"That's something I don't want to talk about," he dryly said as he looked straight forward out of the window.

I watched him as that question caused his body to tense up, for his eyes to become tight and for a mug to appear on his face.

"Jaxsyn," I called his name, and the facial expression he wore was wiped off his face and he was now back to his calm demeanor.

"What's up." He looked at me as if he just didn't zone out.

"What do you want to talk about then?"

"All I want to talk about right now is us. I want you to tell me that when you get off of work, you are going to let me come and pick you up tonight." He smiled at me and even though I was telling myself to say no, I nodded my head to tell him yes.

Yes, I would allow him to come and pick me up, take me to his house, and most likely fuck my damn brains out.

"Speak to me baby girl."

"Yes, Jaxsyn, you can come pick me up later." I rolled my eyes at him.

"Good, well it's time for you to go back to work. I'll be seeing you later." He raised to his feet, pulled his blue jean pants up, then adjusted them low enough for me to see the rim of his red Polo boxers that so happened to match the color of his red and white Jordan's on his feet.

"Come here though." He grabbed me up and pulled me close to him.

"I'm for real sorry about how I snapped at you. I was just in a bad headspace. I'm going to make it up to you tonight," he said as he leaned in and kissed me on the forehead.

My words got stuck in my damn throat as I stood there, soaking up all this attention he was showing me.

"Yeah, whatever." I snapped out of it and pulled away from him.

Jaxsyn chuckled and I secretly smiled too. "You funny. But I'll see you later."

He winked and then walked out of the pizza place and I was still standing there watching him as if he was on a runway. Shaking my head, I jetted out of MOB's and went back to work.

Jaxsyn

I was happy to see Kaizlyn. Her face, when I snapped on her, was imprinted in my brain. I had been wanting to apologize but I had let my pride stop me from knocking on her grandma's door to talk to her. Not to mention the stuff with my sister. She had yet to wake up and the shit was killing me slowly. I lowkey felt like I had failed her. I was supposed to protect her and I let her get too involved with a fuck nigga, and now look at how things were.

Sighing, I hopped off of the elevator with a vase of flowers and a teddy bear to take into her room. Even though her eyes were shut and she probably couldn't hear me, I found a sense of peace by talking to her.

The doctors thought that after her surgery that she would wake up, but she didn't. She had slipped into a coma and I swear I just wanted to set Houston, TX on fire, but what would that solve? Well, let me rephrase that because I planned on getting revenge for this shit. I just wanted to make sure that I was getting the right mothafucker when I did cause hell.

Taking a deep breath, I stopped right in front of her front door before I entered. I closed my eyes, sent a prayer up to God then walked in.

The sight of her not being her loud, annoying self was so fucking heartbreaking.

"Hey baby girl. I brought you some flowers and a teddy bear," I let her know as I sat both of them down in the window.

Walking back over to her bedside, I stood there looking down at her beautiful chocolate face. She was still so pretty. She actually resembled our mother a lot.

Fuck. I turned around and shook my head. This pain here was something I hadn't felt in a long time.

To be real, I had never felt anything like this. This shit hurt worse than the heartache I felt when my mother said fuck us.

Turning back around, I grabbed her hand. "I'm so sorry I wasn't there to protect you. I swear if you make it through this shit, I will never, ever let nothing like this happen again. I've always protected you and this time I failed, miserably. Wake up, Keisha. You have to wake up sis." I leaned forward and kissed my sister on the forehead.

"You're strong. We have been through so much and I know you gon' come through this. I'll be back tomorrow to see you. I love you," I told her.

Running my hands down my face, I left out of the hospital room. When I did go see her, I could only be in there for a couple of minutes. The shit was just too hard and I had to stay strong and get to the bottom of who did this to her. I knew I wasn't going to stop until the person who did it was six feet under.

* * *

AFTER HANGING out with Ace for a little bit and chopping it up with him about some shit and who we thought it was that did that shit to my sister, I had found myself drinking all of my sorrow away.

I was currently standing outside of Kaizlyn's window. I couldn't wait to see her and stick my damn dick up in her ass.

Staggering over to her window, first I knocked lightly but after feeling like she wasn't coming fast enough to the window, I knocked harder as I leaned up against the side of the house.

"Kaizzlllynnn…" I slurred as I pushed myself forward and went back to the window.

"Kaizlynnn," I called her name out again and I tapped on the window.

Finally, with the biggest mug on her face and with her hair all over her head, she was looking out the window at me.

"Jaxsyn," she huffed and rolled her eyes. She was peeking out of the window and I flashed her smile.

"Go to the front," she mouthed and I staggered my way to the front of her porch.

It felt like my head was spinning so I had a seat on the steps then laid my head up against the railing of the steps as I waited for her.

Hearing the front door open, out walked Kaizlyn in a pair of tights and a purple jacket. Her hair was now up into a ponytail and she had on some black boots.

"I thought you were coming earlier. Not this damn late," she fussed.

My intentions were to come and pick her up earlier but I had got so lost in the shots of D'usse that I had lost track of time.

"My bad," were all the words that I could muster up.

Trying to stand to my feet, I found myself leaning backwards and damn near falling off of the stairs.

"Shit, I'm fucked up," I said more to myself but out loud as I ran my hands over the top of my head and gained my composure back.

"I hope you don't think I'm going anywhere with you drunk like this. You can go over to your grandma's and sleep this off and we try again tomorrow," Kaizlyn rambled, but I wasn't trying to hear none of that. I was drunk and I was horny as fuck.

"Man, hush." I waved her off. "I got this. You go get your shit and come and get in the car," I told her, and she looked at me with an evil glare, but she didn't rebel. Instead, she turned quickly on her toes and headed back in the house.

While I waited on her, I went and got back in my car.

Knock! Knock!

The loud knocks on my driver's side window caused me to jump out of my sleep and reach down for my gun.

Looking out of the window, I realized it was Kaizlyn. I must have dozed off while she was getting her shit together.

Shaking my head at myself, I unlocked the door and she walked around the front of the car and came to the passenger side. Kaizlyn got in the car and looked at me crazily upside of my head.

"What ma?"

"I really don't think you should be drinking and driving," she said, sounding concerned, but she didn't have anything to worry about. I had been doing this shit for a minute. Drinking and driving was my thing and all I needed was for her to sit back, relax and let me control this shit.

"I got this," I said boastfully as I started my car, put my foot on the brake then placed my car in drive.

"Jaxsyn, wrong way," she shouted as I began to go backward instead of forward.

"Shit." I looked down and my ass was really fucked up. I hadn't put the car in drive and I had to admit, her ass was right. I was in no condition to be driving.

"You know how to drive?" I looked at her and she gave me the funniest look ever.

"Yeah, but I ain't driving yo' shit."

"Girl, if you don't stop yo' shit. Come and drive Daddy's car. You can sit on my lap and drive if you want to." I laughed and she swatted at me.

"I'm good. The least you can do is get your ass in the back seat and sleep some of that liquor off," she sassed.

"Nah, I need to be in the front seat so I can watch yo' ass in case you don't really know how to drive," I let her know as I reached for the door handle and got out.

Kaizlyn got out of the car too and we met each other in front of the car. Grabbing her up, I cupped her pussy and squeezed it tightly. I could feel the warmness in between her thighs, as I gently rubbed backward and forward. The more I rubbed, the more she became putty in my hands. All the sassy talking, snapping and little slick comments weren't coming out her mouth right now. Yeah, I might have been drunk but that didn't have shit to do with how I could make her ass feel.

"It feels good don't it?" I leaned forward and whispered in her ear.

"Mhmm," she let out as I dipped my hands in her tights and let my fingers slide in between her fat, wet pussy lips.

"Talk to me," I told her as she leaned her head forward and rested on my shoulders. I continued to toy with her pussy.

"Yes, Jaxsyn," she moaned out. She then snatched my hand out of her pants and I smirked.

She rolled her eyes, adjusted her tights then got in the car.

Chuckling, I lifted my fingers up to my nose, inhaling the sweet smell of her pussy juices that were glistening on my finger.

"Drive my shit right or it's your ass." I looked at her out the corner of my eye and she took a deep breath, adjusted the seat and put her seatbelt on. Kaizlyn then placed her foot on the brake and put the car in drive.

She slowly pulled off from in front of her grandma's house and I reached forward and put some music on.

"No, turn that off. I can't listen to that and drive." She looked at me quickly and back at the road.

"Ah hell. What you mean?" I laughed as I turned the music back down. I didn't have time to play with her ass.

"I like to focus on the road without that music playing," she seriously stated, and I swear I thought that was the funniest shit ever.

I was dead ass laughing at her and I could tell by the frown on her face, she wasn't feeling the fact that I thought her statement was funny.

"Do you want me to turn around and go home? And however you get home is all on you?" she asked.

Kaizlyn never took her eyes off of the road as she talked to me.

"Ok. Ok." I threw my hands up. "I quit." I laughed.

She then flashed me a glare which caused her to serve off into another lane. The car that was on the side of us blew their horn!

"Let me stop fuckin' with you before you wreck my shit." I was now serious as I leaned back in the seat and directed Kaizlyn to my house.

Even though she had been there before, she was acting like she didn't remember the way.

Finally pulling up to the front of my house, I stepped outside of the car and the first thing I did was took a piss.

"Eww, you couldn't wait until we got in the house?" She raised her nose up at me and I continued to relieve my damn bladder.

I shook my dick off, stuffed it back in my pants and went and followed Kaizlyn up to my front door.

"Stop acting like you ain't never seen nobody take a piss before." I reached around her and grabbed my keys out of her hand. I then opened the door to my house and scooted her inside as I wrapped my hands around her waist.

"Eww go wash your hands!" she fussed, and I ignored her ass.

I continued to guide her up the stairs and to my bedroom.

Once we entered the room, I stripped out of my clothes. I was going to take a hot ass shower, with hopes it sobered a nigga up.

"What are you doing?" Kaizlyn's eyes were bulging out of her head as she watched me stroke my now hard dick.

"I'm going to take a shower. You wanna join me?" I asked her with my eyebrow raised.

"Nah, I'm good." She sat down on the bed and I shrugged.

I walked into the bathroom, cut the shower on then got in. The hot water felt good as fuck.

Grabbing my men's soap, I began to cleanse myself. With my head down, I was letting the water pour over my head when I heard the sliding door to the shower open.

There in her birthday suit stood Kaizlyn. She had taken off all her clothes and had also let her long, pretty hair down. It was falling over her shoulders and was almost hovering over her perfectly round breasts.

Standing there, it was as if the lights were shining directly down on her. Her skin was glowing and I was feeling my dick get harder and harder the longer I stared at her pretty ass.

"Come here." I fingered for her.

With her hands covering her breasts, she slowly walked over to me and entered the shower with me. It was as if my hands were magnets and she was metal as they gravitated and began to have a mind of their own. Her body was just as soft as I remembered it to be the last time we had fucked around.

"Damn." I licked my lips. I gently touched her beautiful ass face, as I let my fingers glide from her face to the sides of her neck which made her jump a little. I then slowly tickled the sides of her rib cage which made her giggle.

"That tickles." She wiggled in my embrace.

"You're so damn beautiful Kaizlyn," I said lowly as the water bounced off of me and splashed onto her.

"Thank you." She bashfully smiled at me.

I swear to God, Kaizlyn was fucking pretty. She was a naturally pretty girl but I felt like she had forgotten.

Grabbing her round face, I pulled her in close to me and stared into her pretty ass eyes and kissed her. I kissed her so damn roughly that she couldn't help but back up a little, but that didn't cause our embrace to break. I stuck my tongue in her mouth as she let her hands roam up and down my body. Her soft touch felt good against my damn skin, or maybe it was the damn alcohol that had my body sensitive to everything.

"Fuck Kaizlyn," I moaned against her lips before I bit down on her bottom lip.

"What Jaxsyn?" She looked up at me with the sexiest look that one could muster up. She just looked so innocent, but I knew deep down she wasn't.

"Bend over." I grabbed the back of her neck roughly, but not in a way to hurt her.

Not even giving her the chance to protest, I bent her over my damn self, causing her to cry out.

"Ahh," she yelled out as I spread her ass cheeks apart and stuffed my dick off into her juicy pussy.

"Damn Kaizlyn. This shit will have a nigga going crazy." I grabbed her by her small waist as I jammed my dick deeper off into her.

"Jaxsyn..." she moaned out as her hands rested on the slippery, wet wall.

"What ma? Talk to me," I said as I continued to find that one spot that would have her ass going crazy.

"I can't standdd..." she whined. "I'm going to fall." She tried to keep her balance but her legs began to shake the harder I pounded into her center, causing her to lose her balance and damn near collapse.

"Nah, stand up and take this dick." I lifted her half limp body up and pressed it up against the steamy, wet wall. I yanked her hands above her head and pinned them together.

The hot, steamy water cascaded off of our bodies as I lifted her right leg up and positioned it on the edge of the tub.

Now that I had more room to enter her, I filled her body back up with all nine inches of me. Which instantly caused Kaizlyn to gasp and claw at the wall.

Her eyes began to roll into the back of her head as her face scrunched up from the pleasure I was delivering her. I was trying to snatch her soul with this dick because I could feel her snatching mine.

Kaizlyn's ass didn't know how much power she had in between her legs. She could have it all if she asked me. I could see me trying to change her whole world but I knew that with her being young, I had to take things slowly.

"Jaxsyn, baby, right there..." she moaned as I began to circle my dick inside of her.

"Oh my god... Please stop... Please," she begged of me, but I wasn't letting up.

Smacking her on the ass, it caused for droplets to splash everywhere. "Take this dick Kaizlyn. I know you like the way it makes you feel. I can tell by the look on your face."

"You like how it feel baby?" I asked her as I grabbed her neck, forcing her to look me in the face.

Her love faces were driving me crazy as she bit down on her lip, scrunched up her nose and closed her eyes.

"Kaizlyn, talk to me. How does it feel?"

"It feels..." As she was trying to get her words out, I went deep. So deep that I knew she felt that shit in her stomach.

"Ahh," she moaned loudly. "I'm cuming... Ahh," she sang, and I could feel her pussy tighten around my dick. It felt like it was sucking me in deeper and deeper.

"Shit," I hissed as I gripped her hips and nutted all inside of her.

My toes popped and my stomach tightened up as I let off a big ass load. Now my ass felt like I was about to tumble down to the ground. That nut, mixed with the number of drinks I had, had me feeling light-headed. I knew I was going to sleep good as fuck after this.

Pulling my limp dick out of her, my nut, which was also mixed with her juices, began to flow up out of her as she held on to the wall for dear life. She was still breathing heavy and her eyes were still closed.

"Let me wash you off, then we can go get in the bed." I lifted her up and pulled her close to me. My dick was beginning to rise again which caused her to look up at me.

Shaking her head, no, I laughed because she looked so drained and tired.

"You tired?" I chuckled as I grabbed the bar of soap, lathered it up in my hand then placed it back.

I began massaging over her body as I cleaned her. Sticking my hands between her legs, I massaged slowly back and forth and I could feel how swollen it was from the steamy sex we had just had.

After we finished taking a shower together, we dried off and got in the bed butt ass naked and as soon as our heads hit the pillow, we were both knocked out.

Whoodie

$\mathcal{I}$t was Sunday afternoon and I was currently thinking about how my family and friends had to get together to have a memorial for all of my homies and friends that I had lost due to Jaxsyn. Guilt had grabbed my heart in a choke hold when I had to watch everyone grieve over something so unfortunate, and it only made me want revenge even more. Not to mention my right-hand man was still laid up in the hospital trying to recover thanks to that bitch, Keisha.

I was thankful that Sims was doing better and making progress but he wasn't in the clear just yet. Him being stabbed in the neck was requiring different types of surgery, not to mention, he had just gotten shot in the arm by Keisha.

Shaking my head, I couldn't believe that one person had fucked Sims up like that.

"So, you say that nigga be there every Sunday?" I asked Dex who was sitting next to me.

We were currently sitting in the new club that my uncle had just opened up. He had been laying low after some shit had happened months ago, and he had decided that he was finally ready to step back on the scene with a night club. He didn't want to jump back into the drug game just yet because he knew he had a lot of eyes on him after he was accused of murdering his girlfriend.

See, my uncle had been down here in Texas for some years. So long that he no longer had his Louisiana accent and it was only certain words that would ease off his tongue that would let you know that he was from there.

"Yup, he hasn't missed a day yet. Lowkey, that nigga be looking at me funny and shit, but he hadn't said nothing to me." Dex shrugged because I knew his ass didn't give a fuck.

Dex was a real ass nigga that lived by a G-code. He was always down for the ride and would bust a nigga's ass if you asked him to. He was a real one and since Sims was out of commission and would be for a while, I was about to let Dex have his spot so we could make a move on that nigga Jaxsyn.

"You want to make that move today?" I looked up at him and he smirked.

"I'm ready whenever you are."

"Bet." I nodded. "Say ma, give me a drink." This fine ass bitch came from around the corner of the bar.

She was a dark chick with long blonde hair and a big booty. She looked to be older than me but that had never stopped me from getting a bitch that I had laid eyes on.

"Excuse me?" She cocked her head to the side and mugged me.

Off the muscle, I already knew what type of chick she was. She was feisty with a bad attitude, and that was only because she thought that made her ass look cuter.

"You heard me."

"Let me see your ID?" She came and stood in front of me as she leaned against the bar and eyed me up and down.

"Man, get out of here. Give me a drink," I let her know again.

"I can't serve you if you don't show me your ID." She tapped her long, claw-like nails against the bar, she then held her hand out, waiting for me to put my ID in her hand.

"He good." My uncle walked from the back of the building and over to where we were.

"Oh, I'm sorry boss." She quickly submitted the moment that my uncle made his presence known.

"It's all good," my uncle told her as I stood to my feet to greet him.

Lowkey, he was who I wanted to be like. He was and still is one of the biggest drug dealers that I knew. That nigga ran shit when he was in Louisiana and when he got to Texas, he marked his lil' territory real quick. He snatched up a lot of areas and that's exactly what I wanted to do.

I wanted to take over and be like him. I wanted to be able to walk around and get the respect that I knew that I deserved. But first things first, I had to get these niggas to understand I wasn't one to be played with. I had fucked up because I had let that nigga Jaxsyn get away with too much already. I honestly felt like he thought that he could test me and toy with me because I was younger than him but shit, age didn't mean shit in these streets and I was going to prove that shit to his ass. Once I killed him and took over his blocks.

"How is everything going my boy? What y'all want to drink?" my uncle Ted asked me as we dabbed each other up and brought it in with a hug.

"It doesn't matter to me," Dex replied.

"Shit, give me whatever you have that's brown and I'm just trying to be like you," I truthfully told him.

Chuckling, he sat down next to me. "Londyn, get us three Jacks on easy ice," he demanded the chick who had given me a hard time.

I watched as she scurried to make the drinks and when she handed them back to us, I winked at her.

"So, you trying to be like your old uncle, huh?" He picked up his drink and took a sip from it.

"Hell yeah," I let him know.

"That'll take hard work and no bullshittin'." He looked at me out the corner of his eyes.

"I'm not out here bullshittin'. I'm just trying to figure it all out, that's all."

"Shit, not by letting some nigga take out your men." He looked sternly at me and I should have known that this was coming.

"I didn't know he was going to fucking come at me so damn hard." I shook my head thinking about the homies that I had to say goodbye to, all because I wasn't ahead of the fucking game.

"That's how I know you not ready to be like me because see, I'm always ten steps ahead of everything," he bragged.

"What do I need to do then?" I asked his advice because I knew he wouldn't lead me in the wrong direction. I knew he would tell me exactly what I should do and how I should do it.

"Simple. End the nigga," he said calmly as he finished off his drink.

"And who is this lil' nigga anyways?" he asked.

"An older nigga name Jaxsyn," I let him know as the chick who had served us paused. She was wiping the top of the bar off but the moment I mentioned Jaxsyn, she stopped.

"You good?" I looked down at her and she turned slowly and looked at me.

"Yeah. Why wouldn't I be?" she sassed as she finished rubbing the top of the bar in a circular motion, getting up all of the wet spot stains from where drinks had been sitting.

"Just checking, but come here really quick." I motioned for her to come down to where I was.

"I think I know who you talking about but of course I'm going to do a little research." My uncle nodded then stood to his feet.

"Aye Londyn, whatever they get is on the house," he let the chick know, and she nodded her head and gave him a big ass smile.

My uncle then said his goodbyes and headed up the stairs that led to his office.

"Now back to you." I rubbed my chin as I glared at her. I was trying to pick up her vibes.

"What do you want with me? Another drink?" Her attitude was so fucking funky and I knew all she needed was for a nigga like me to get that shit in line, because it was obvious the nigga she was fucking with wasn't handling that shit right.

"Nah, I want to talk to you. Is that a problem?" I questioned her.

"No, but I charge for conversion." She rubbed her fingers together and let out a loud ass chuckle.

"Baby, you'll be trying to pay me for conversation and my time if I stick this dick off in you," I said, causing Dex to burst out laughing.

"Nigga you wild. But check it, I got to get out of here. Hit my line with the plans." He stood up and we dabbed it up.

"Bet," I told him then focused my attention back onto the chocolate drop that was standing in front of me.

"Are you going to let me get your number or what?" I licked my lips then smirked, showing off the gold that usually made all the bitches go crazy anyway.

Just like I knew she would, her body relaxed and she took her phone out.

"Give me your number and I'll hit you up," she stated, but little did she know she wasn't running shit.

"Nah ma. Give me your fucking phone and let me put my number in there then call my phone." I yanked her phone out of her hand and began to key my number into her phone. I then called my phone and once it rang one time, I ended the call and gave her back her phone.

"I'll be hitting you up soon." I winked at her and she rolled her eyes and walked off.

It was funny because I could tell that she was putting a little extra bounce in her walk to make that fat ass of hers shake, but little did she know, I was going to fuck all that attitude she was giving me up out of here. It would be long gone and she would be on a nigga's dick hard as fuck.

* * *

"NEXT TIME YOU SEE ME, you not gon' be giving me all that attitude are you?" I smacked Londyn's right ass cheek and I delivered nine inches of dick off into her fat ass pussy.

"Oh my god. No. I'm not," she whimpered as she buried her head into the pillow and bit down on it.

"That's what I thought," I boasted as I rammed into her so damn hard, that you could hear my balls smacking up against her skin.

After I left my uncle's club, I had shot her a text and of course, her ass was giving me that stank ass attitude but the moment I began to speak that real nigga game to her, she gave in, which was why she was at my crib, letting me beat her walls down. She had got off at two in the morning and here it was almost four o'clock and I was still knocking her walls down.

I couldn't lie, her shit was fire. It was wet, tight and the head that she had given me earlier had a nigga seeing stars. No doubt, she was a pro and knew what she was doing. The more she threw her ass back, the tighter she would grip her pussy around my dick.

Fucking her wasn't like fucking the girls my age. Don't get me wrong, I had fucked plenty of bitches. A nigga been on bitches since I was thirteen years old. Even though I was seventeen, a nigga had been getting it out the trenches and the swamps of Louisiana. I had seen the good and the bad already.

Being in Louisiana, you could lose your homie at the age of ten. You had to learn how to survive and when I moved to Texas, I had totally let my guard down and got caught slippin'.

"Fuck me harder Daddy," Londyn cooed as she reached back, spread her own ass cheeks apart, wanting me to go deeper.

I was now balls deep, with my thumb in her ass, giving her exactly what she had asked of me. To go harder. I was going so hard that I had knocked her ass all the way up to the headboard.

"Yes. Yes. Yes," she screamed as she began to cream all over my dick.

My dick was starting to swell as the nut I was ready to bust rushed to the head of my dick and with one more deep stroke, I let all my seeds go inside of the condom.

Pulling out, I fell to the side of her and she stayed in the same position. Londyn had her ass in the air as she tried to catch her breath.

Sitting up, I smacked her on the ass then got out of the bed to go flush the condom down the toilet, wash my dick off and wash my hands.

"Aye, some girl name Chyna is calling your phone," she hollered from the bedroom.

What the fuck is she doing calling me this damn late? I wondered.

See, Chyna had been slowly losing her damn mind. It was like if I wasn't up under her she would throw fits, cry and just do the most. I felt like I fucked her ass so good and now she didn't want to leave me alone. Her ass was even missing school and shit.

Yeah, at first it was cool because I knew that I didn't have to really be around her like that because she stayed a little minute away from me, so that meant there was no chance of us bumping into each other or me getting caught being with Keisha but shit, the more dick I gave her the more she started coming around. Shit was weird and I was going to let her know what was up.

"Aite," I hollered back.

After drying my hands off, I went back into the bedroom and laid down while Londyn went into the bathroom to take a shower. I normally would make bitches leave, but I wanted to hit that pussy again when I woke up.

The moment I heard Londyn cut the shower on, I checked my phone and saw that Chyna had been calling my ass.

Sighing, I decided to call her to see what she wanted. Just maybe it was an emergency or some shit.

"What's good?" I asked her the moment she answered the phone.

"Oh my god. Why haven't you been answering my calls?" she whined into the phone, and I just knew that she was about to be on that extra shit.

"I've been busy. Why you up at this time of night though?" I questioned.

The day that shit happened to Sims, I had told myself that I was done with school. I had dropped the fuck out and I didn't give a fuck. They were lucky I had made it this far. College was not in my plans and high school wasn't doing anything but taking up my time when I could be out hustling in the streets. Making sure that I'm making the right moves and not getting caught slippin'.

However, that was my decision. Yeah, I had told Chyna that I was through with school but when I said that shit, that didn't mean her dumb ass was supposed to drop out right along with me.

"I miss you and I don't care about school. I just want to be under you baby," she chimed and I exhaled.

Shaking my head, I sat up in the bed and ran my hand down my face.

"You trippin' Chyna, baby. You don't do what I do. You do better than me," I let her know as I heard the shower cut off.

"But I want to see you. I'm outside," she blurted out.

"Hey Daddy, you got another towel?" Londyn yelled from the bathroom, and I just knew Chyna heard her.

"Who the fuck is that?" she shouted into the phone as I placed my hand over the speaker and cursed.

"Fuck." I placed the phone on mute then answered Londyn, "Yeah, hold up."

"Whoodie... Whoodie are you fucking serious? Let me fucking in your house," she was shouting on the phone.

I took the phone off of mute when I walked out of the room and into the other guest bedroom to get a towel.

"Chill out. It's not what you think," I lied to her.

"If it's not what I think, then let me in," she stated. "If you don't let me in, I'll just bang on your door until you do," she said in a matter of fact tone.

"Go home Chyna," I said sternly but seconds later, I could hear banging on my front door. She was banging so hard that I was pretty sure it would wake the fucking neighbors.

"Fuck," I cursed as I went back into the room and made my way to the bathroom so I could give Londyn her towel.

"Is everything ok?" she asked as she wrapped the towel around her body which caused my dick to wake up and want to fuck her ass again.

"Yeah. I just gotta handle some shit real quick," I let her know as I walked over to my dresser, slipped on a pair of basketball shorts, no underwear or t-shirt and headed out of the room.

Once I reached the front door, I yanked it open then closed it back. I yanked Chyna up and pinned her up in the corner of the porch as I held my hands around her neck.

"Didn't I tell you to take your ass home?" I said lowly but sternly in her ear.

"But Whoodie... I wanted to spend time with you. Why do you have another bitch in there? You smell like another bitch," she shouted as tears began to escape her eyes.

Chyna had me so heated with her theatrics, that I wasn't even fazed by the cold night's air and I hoped she knew that no matter how hard she cried, she wasn't coming into my house. She was about to get in her car and go home.

"Chyna, I don't want to have to do this with cha. Take ya ass home." I stepped away from her and she looked at me like she hated my guts right now.

Swinging, Chyna hit me in my chest and I snapped. Before I knew it, I had backhanded her, which caused her to hold her face and look at me in disbelief. Me hitting her had shocked her so much, that she wasn't even crying no more.

"Really Whoodie?" she mouthed.

"Just go," I told her.

We both stood there staring at each other. Finally, Chyna broke eye contact, pushed past me and stormed off to her car. When she got in her car, she slammed her own car door and zoomed out of my yard.

Shaking my head, I went back into the house and made a mental note to apologize to her ass tomorrow.

"Is everything good now or do I need to go?" Londyn was sitting on the bed wrapped in the towel that I had given her.

"Oh no, you good. I handled it." I climbed in the bed and pulled her up to where I was.

We then cuddled up together like we had been fucking with each other for a minute. Moments later, I could hear her light snores and I closed my eyes and joined her.

Chyna

ou're such a dumb bitch. You are so fucking dumb. Just dumb. Dumb! I cried to myself as I drove back home.

I couldn't believe Whoodie. I mean, let me stop. How couldn't I? Look at the shit that he had already done. I should have known better. I had watched him treat that other girl he was with like shit. So, what made me think I was any different?

Hell, the moment he made me leave a party to be with her, I should have known better, but my extra dumb ass didn't.

Shaking my head, I sniffled as I wiped away the tears that I had been crying.

I should just leave him alone, I told myself, but it was way easier said than done. Even after what had just happened between us, I was waiting for the moment he texted my phone to tell me that he was sorry for putting his hands on me.

Ugh, I sighed as I picked up my phone. I wanted to let Whoodie know how I felt. I needed him to know that I hated his fucking guts.

Me: I fucking hate you. I can't believe you played me like that and the fact that you put your hands on me, let's me know that you just a trash ass nigga. I should have known better and that's why Jaxsyn's boss ass is going to fucking merk you.

I pressed send on the message and then locked my phone back. Yes, I was speaking from anger and a confused heart.

Picking my phone back up, I unlocked my phone and reread the message that I had sent him.

"Shit," I pouted, wishing that I could take the message back because I knew that last part was going to piss him off, especially due to the circumstances.

"Fuck, fuck, fuck…" I began to bite down on my nails as I thought of another text that I could send him in order to possibly save my ass.

Instead of texting him back apologizing for my choice of words, I locked my phone back and sat it in my lap and focused on the road.

Ding!

Hearing the sound of my phone going off caused my heart to drop. I felt like I was having a mini heart attack. I was damn near scared to open up my phone and read the message that Whoodie had sent back.

Inhaling, I held my breath as I unlocked my phone and went to the message icon. Seeing that it was Melo, I exhaled and opened up his message.

Melo: Thinking of you.

Reading over his message made me smile. It also made me think and compare the two of them. I had left Melo alone for a nigga that didn't even have the balls to respect me, but what did I think I was going to get from his thug ass?

Me: Wanna come over or meet in our spot?

I sent him a text back, then zoned out as I drove to my house. I needed to keep my mind off Whoodie, so why not have someone to do it?

Melo: Is your mom home?

Me: Now, you know she is out somewhere doing God knows what.

I texted him back as I pulled into my yard. It was the truth though. There was no telling where my mom was. She had been at home a little too long anyways. I knew that it was way past due for her to hit the streets again.

Melo: Bet. I'm on my way.

Me: Ok. Just let yourself in.

After texting him back, I got out of the car and entered the house. I went upstairs to my room and went into the bathroom to see how bad my face looked from Whoodie slapping me.

Damn, I sighed as I let my fingers glide over the bruise I had on my face.

Pulling out my drawer, I put a little powder makeup on it so that Melo wouldn't be asking me questions, then left out the bathroom and went and had a seat on my bed.

About fifteen minutes later, I could hear Melo's car pull up in my yard and then I heard the front door close. Moments later, he was walking through my room door, in a pair of grey sweats, a grey hoodie and some Nike slides on his feet.

"Why are you even up?" I asked him.

We were both up like it was the weekend and as if we didn't have school in just a few hours.

"Shit, I couldn't sleep. I got a lot on my mind," Melo chimed as he walked farther into my room and found a seat next to me on the bed.

"Yeah. I feel you. I have a lot on my mind too." I sighed as a quick replay of tonight's events went through my head.

Melo picked my head up and turned me to look at him. "You want to talk about it?"

"Nah, I just want to lay down," I told him truthfully.

I didn't want to talk to my ex about my new boy toy that was putting his hands on me, sleeping with other girls, and driving me wild. That was just a topic I would rather not discuss with him. All I needed from him, was for him to hold me tight in arms tonight as I fell asleep. For him to just give a sense of security.

"I just want to lay next to you, if that is ok?" I looked him in his eyes and he tilted his head as he looked at me.

Melo reached his hand out towards my face, and he let his hands caress the side of my face that held the bruise from being slapped by Whoodie.

I didn't want to but I flinched, which alerted Melo and he stood to his feet and grabbed me by my arm to yank me to my feet.

"What happened to you?" He looked closely.

"Nothing. It's nothing." I tried to walk away from him but he jerked me back causing me to fall into his chest.

"Chyna, what the fuck. What is going on with you? You losing your damn mind right now. You out here letting someone put their hands on you?" he asked me in a heated tone, and what was I supposed to say?

I mean, I could tell him the truth but lowkey, I was too embarrassed to. One being, that my feelings for Whoodie were what made me put Melo in the friend zone and I didn't want him to know all of the shit I was having to put up with. Second, I was truthfully settling for less. I had downgraded.

"Melo, it's nothing. Now can we lay down, or you can go." I folded my arms and rolled my eyes.

"I mean, it's whatever. We can lay down but listen to me." He cuffed my chin and raised my head to look at him.

"Yeah, we just friends Chyna, but if you need me to beat a nigga's ass for you, I got you," he stated confidently, and I wanted to burst out laughing in his face.

Yeah, Melo was that nigga at the school we went to but when it came to Whoodie, he was no match, because even though Melo would have thought they would box that shit out like normal people, Whoodie would just pull out a gun and shoot his ass. So yes, it was cute of Melo to say that shit, but it was all in vain because I knew that it wouldn't be a fair fight.

"I hear you Melo, but I'm tired." I pulled away from him and got in my bed.

Melo stood there shaking his head, then he slipped his shoes off and got in the bed behind me.

* * *

"WHAT DO you two think you are doing? Why aren't you at school?" My mother barged into my room and I popped up out of my sleep. Melo sat up too and he was looking like all the blood had drained out of his face.

"Mom, why are you even trippin'? It's Melo, not some random guy," I told her.

Any other time she wouldn't even too much care. She loved Melo and me together.

"Whatever, and that was before you felt like you could skip school every day. Get up and get dressed and go to school. The both of you," she spat as she eyed me up and down, then looked over at Melo.

The way she looked at him was weird as fuck and her whole attitude about him being here caught me off guard.

When she slammed my door as if she was an angry teenager, I sighed as I picked up my phone and checked the time. Realizing that I had enough time to get dressed and make it to the first period, I locked my phone back so that I could get up.

"What is her issue?" Melo asked as he got out of the bed and headed to the bathroom.

"I don't know." I rolled my eyes.

I quickly washed my face and brushed my teeth and Melo did the same. He had an extra toothbrush at my house from when he used to come over all the time.

He had decided that he could wear what he already had on because he had slipped it on when he took a shower last night, and all I did was slip on a pair of jeans and a black t-shirt with a pair of black boots. I grabbed my backpack and jacket and we walked downstairs to where my mother was sitting in the living room.

She had the ugliest look on her face. Like she was irritated about something.

"Mom, what's wrong?" I asked her as I held the doorknob, getting ready to open it. Melo was standing behind me, looking straight ahead as if he would get in trouble if he turned his head and looked at her.

"Girl, get out of here." She waved me off as if I had done something wrong.

"And Melo, you can't speak." She looked at him and he stared blankly at her.

"Hey Ms. Jade." He quickly waved. He was acting really nervous around her like this was their first time meeting each other.

"Hey Melo baby, and next time, speak." She raised her eyebrow up at him and seductively spoke to him. Melo nodded his head slowly as he darted his eyes from her to me.

"Uhm ok. Bye Mom. I'll see you later." I looked awkwardly at the two of them and left out the door with Melo damn near running me over me trying to get out of my house.

"What the hell was that about?" I questioned him, and he shrugged his shoulders.

He and she had never acted that awkwardly around each other and I wondered if it had to do with my dealings with a new man. I knew that my mother liked Melo for me. I just hoped that she wasn't up to something or that she had him watching out for me.

"Well, I guess I will see you at school." I reached my car and rested against the driver's side door.

"Ok. See you there." He smiled at me and then headed for his car.

As he looked back at me, he darted his eyes to the window then turned back around quickly. I turned my head to see what he was looking at and there peeping out of the window was my nosey ass mom, so I waved and she quickly closed the blinds.

I shook my head and got in my car. I put my keys in the ignition and backed out of the driveway and began to follow behind Melo as he headed to school.

Melo

$\mathscr{I}$ swear, I felt like my life couldn't get any more complicated, but it had. The moment that I had let Chyna's mom put my dick in her mouth, she had been sweating me ever since. She had been texting me letting me know how much she wanted my dick back down her throat.

Her ass was an old freak and I couldn't lie, she could suck the fuck out some dick, but I wasn't trying to make it a habit. I wasn't trying to go there with her again with the chances of me and Chyna maybe getting back together.

When I texted Chyna last night, or should I say this morning, I wasn't expecting her to text a nigga back. She was just on my mind and I wanted to let her know. But when she did text me back asking if I wanted to meet up with her, I jumped on that shit. Chyna was a cool ass female when she wasn't on no dumb ass shit. And ever since we had started dating, I had only been around her moms a few times because her ass was always gone, and I had honestly expected for her to be gone when I came, but I got the surprise of my life when she walked up into Chyna's room. I didn't even know what to expect. I knew she wouldn't say anything because then that would ruin her relationship with her daughter.

But the shit was definitely fucking weird as fuck. I was sweating fucking bullets and my ass was nervous. If Chyna would have been close to me, she would have heard my damn heart beating as loud as a fucking drum.

Ding!

Hearing my phone go off caused me to look down and grab it out of my lap. Unlocking it, I read over the message and regret began to run through my whole body.

Fuck. I shook my head as message after message began to come in on my phone. It was Chyna's mom, expressing to me on how upset she was with me being there laid up with her daughter after what we had shared together. The shit was crazy as fuck to read because we didn't even have a special moment. All she did was suck my dick and that was it.

As I continued to read, the more and more my phone would go off. It was fucking blowing me. *Like, what the fuck is wrong with her?* I wondered.

The last message that I received was the one that damn near made me run into a different lane.

"What the fuck she meant by she's going to tell Chyna?" I read over the message out loud.

Looking from the road then back down at my phone, I tried to focus on both things. Quickly texting her back, I let her know that I would meet up with her later on.

She had told me she wanted me to meet her after school at Vermont Hotel and that if I didn't, she would text her daughter and let her know what me and her had done. That shit puzzled the fuck out of me because I didn't think that she would do something so low like that, but I guess I was wrong.

I mean, I had to remind myself that Chyna's mother never really showed me that she cared about her daughter. She was always gone and Chyna basically did what the fuck she wanted to do. And honestly, her mother never really showed her motherly love. Well, at least I had never witnessed it, so I should have known that she wouldn't care.

The moment she stuck my dick in her mouth when she knew that I had and was fucking with her daughter, should have been my first sign that she didn't give a fuck. I should have snatched my dick back and got the fuck out of there, but now the shit was already done. I couldn't take it back and unless I wanted her to expose my ass to Chyna, I was going to have to follow her rules until I could figure this shit out.

Finally pulling into the school parking lot, I swooped into an empty parking spot and Chyna parked right beside me. Cutting my car off, I sat there trying to get my thoughts together and process everything.

Knocking on my window, right as my phone dinged again, it was like the sweat instantly began to form on my forehead as Chyna waited for me to get out the car.

I ignored the text message, placed my phone on vibrate and got out the car. Looking up at me, Chyna smiled brightly at me and I forced a fake smile back. I felt like the most fucked up person on planet earth. With all the secrets that I was having to keep inside of me, I knew that I would evidently drive myself fucking crazy.

"You ok?" she asked me as we walked up to the school together.

"Yeah, I'm good," I replied as I felt my phone vibrate inside of my pocket.

We then entered the school and went our separate ways, rushing, trying to make sure we made it to second period before the bell rang.

TIME HAD FLOWN BY. I mean, I had been watching the clock down to the very second, hoping that it would slow down. But I was now walking out of the school doors and to my surprise, Chyna was posted up on the hood of my car, looking down at her phone.

"What's up?" I asked her once I approached her.

"Nothing, just wanted to see if you wanted to hang out or something." She looked up at me.

Even though I wanted to hang with her, I had to turn her down. There was no way in hell that I would stand her mother up knowing that she was making the kind of threats that she was.

"We can after I handle some shit for my mother," I lied to her, and I was hoping she didn't pick up on it.

"Ahh, ok. Well, text me when you're done doing whatever it is. I'll be at home." She stood up, then came and gave me a hug.

"Alright." I hugged her back and I began to feel more and more like shit.

"And Melo, thank you for being a friend and being here for me," she stated.

Fuck, I thought. She just had to give me even more of a reason to feel like a fuck nigga.

"No problem Chyna. You already know what it is," I told her as my phone began to vibrate against my leg, and I knew for a fact she felt it too.

"Who is that?" she asked as I took the phone out of my pocket and ignored the call that was coming in.

"Oh, I don't know. I don't know the number," I lied even more as I slipped the phone back into my pocket. "But look, I got to go. I'll text you later and see if you free, ok."

"Alright. Bye Melo." She waved me goodbye as she walked over to her car and got in.

I didn't want her following me, so I sat in my car and waited until she drove out of the parking lot. Once she was gone, I pulled the address up to the hotel and put in my GPS. It showed that I was only twenty minutes away, so I crept slowly out of the school parking lot and headed to meet up with Chyna's mom to see what exactly she wanted. I was also going to try to let her know that what she thought was going to keep happening was going to get nipped in the bud today, because this shit was foul on so many different occasions.

Exactly like the GPS said, it was now twenty minutes later and I was pulling up to this nice ass hotel building. Parking my car, far away from the entrance, I shot Chyna's mom a text to let her know that I was here and for her to tell me the room number.

832-8986-3654: Room number 365, the door is open. I'm waiting for you.

Reading over the text, I got out of the car and looked around me. I was checking out my surroundings and was hoping like hell that nobody I knew from school or around town saw me.

Entering the automatic doors, I was greeted by Joy, a girl that I went to high school with, and I wanted so badly to keep on walking but I had to keep my cool.

"Hey Melo, what you doing here?" she asked.

"Shit, none of your business. Why are you here? How are you able to work here?" I questioned her, because I knew that we had just got out of school.

"I have double early release and I am eighteen," she stated as if I was the dumb one and should have known. She also rolled her eyes.

Joy never really too much cared for me after all that shit that had gone down with me and Kaizlyn. Especially because Kaizlyn hadn't talked to her since the day that I had broken up with her.

"Yeah ok," I dryly replied as I walked over to the elevator and pressed the number three. As I stood there and waited for the doors to open, I stuck my hands in my pockets and looked around at the pictures that were on the wall. Not that I cared about the images, but I didn't want to make any more eye contact with anybody else.

The doors finally opened and I hopped on as it slowly took me up to the third floor. Hearing the dinging noise, the doors opened and I headed down to room 365.

Once I reached the door, I took a deep breath and then entered. When I walked in, my eyes damn near rolled out of my head. This crazy ass woman had rose petals all over the floor of the hotel room, she had candles lit and sheets sprawled out on the bed, in a lingerie set that was cut out in the middle. Her pussy was on full display and so was her breast.

Turning around, I faced the door and covered my eyes. I didn't know why, but I felt like I wasn't even supposed to be looking her damn near naked body.

"Turn back around and look at me," she seductively commanded of me.

"Nah, I don't think we should be doing this," I let her know with my back still turned to her.

"What Chyna doesn't know can't hurt her and as long as you please me, I won't tell her," she said, and I huffed.

"What you mean? This is crazy," I replied, not being able to believe her choice in words.

"Just turn and look at me, and I bet you change your mind."

Turning around, my eyes widened as I watched Chyna's thirty-some-thing-year-old mother, grab on her breast with her right hand and dip her left hand into her pussy. She was moaning and playing with herself, and I would be a fool if I said that it wasn't turning me on.

My dick would jump every time she stuck her fingers into her pussy. I hated that it had a mind of its own and right now, it was telling me to dig right off into her old ass guts.

"Come here, baby," she moaned as she rubbed her pussy, and I could hear the wetness from across the room.

It was like her words were a magical spell because my feet started moving and I was now sitting on the edge of the bed watching her. As she continued to please herself, she looked me dead in my eyes, licked her lips and let out a moan that turned me on something serious.

Fuck. I knew that once I stuck my dick in her that it would be no turning back, but she was making my ass horny.

"You want to taste me?" She pulled her fingers out of her pussy and they were coated with her cream.

"Nah." I shook my head.

"You sure?" she asked again, and I shook my head no again.

She then stuck her fingers in her mouth and hummed as if that was the best-tasting thing she had ever tasted before in her life.

"I want you to fuck me. I want you to fuck me good." She licked her lips.

"Man, I can't do this." I got up and began to walk towards the door.

Jumping to her feet, Jade pulled at my shirt then ran in front of me.

"Fuck me or I'm calling her right now." She rested her hands on my chest and stared into my eyes.

This lady had to be losing her mind. "You serious?"

"Do it look like I'm playing?" She stepped back and spun around, showing off her nice ass body.

Sighing, I stepped away from her. I walked over to the bed and signaled for her to come. Like a little high school girl, she was chipper as fuck as she made her way to me.

Grabbing her by the back of her neck, I slung her ass down on the bed and when she looked up at me, I could tell by the way her eyes flashed with excitement that she loved that aggressive shit.

I began to take off my clothes and once I was butt ass naked, Cynthia tucked her bottom lip between her teeth and scooted to the middle of the bed, with her legs wide open.

I felt forced to do this but that didn't stop my dick from getting hard. Stroking my dick, I climbed in bed between her legs. "You got a condom?" I asked her, because I sure the fuck didn't have one.

"No, it's ok. I can't have no more kids," she stated, so I placed my dick at her entrance.

She gasped the moment I stuck my dick inside of her. I wasn't even about to try to take things slowly with her. I was going to fuck her so hard and rough with hopes that she wouldn't want to fuck anymore.

Kaizlyn

The week had flown by and it was now the weekend again. To my surprise, Jaxsyn and I had been doing great. He wasn't spazzing out and we actually agreed today that he would take me up there to see his sister.

I hadn't seen her since the day that I had ran out of that party, and I just wanted to go up there so that I could see her. Tomorrow wasn't promised and I just didn't want to continue to let days go by without seeing her.

I was now in my room, searching for my other brown shoe that I wanted to wear. After looking under my bed and even in my closet, I pulled out the suitcases that I had packed my clothes in and searched through them.

Finding the shoe, I smiled and placed it on my feet. I also found the piece of paper that I had written the group home number on and opened it. I sat down on the bed, and I sighed because I hadn't called Emma like I said I would. That made me feel like a bad friend.

With the piece of paper in my hand, I went to the front room and grabbed the house phone. I dialed the number on the piece of paper and listened to the other end as it rang.

"Hello," Mrs. Renee answered, and I smiled.

"Hey Mrs. Renee, can I talk to Emma?" I asked her.

"Oh my, is this Kaizlyn?" she beamed into the phone, and I smiled before I answered.

"Yes, this is her."

"Hey, honey. How is everything going? Are you liking it there?" she asked me.

"Yes. It's not that bad. I really do like it," I truthfully answered.

"That's good. Well, let me go get Emma. I know she can't wait to hear from you," she stated into the phone, and then the line went quiet.

"Hello, Kaizlyn. Kaizlyn is it you?" Emma sounded so excited and I smiled.

"Yeah. It's me. How is everything going over there?"

"It's still the same old stuff, ya know? I miss you and I wish I could come and visit." Her voice echoed sadly throughout the phone and I began to wonder if I could get Mrs. Renee to let her come and visit me for a weekend.

"Maybe we should ask Mrs. Renee and see what she says," I told her, giving her hope.

"Yeah, we should. So, what's new?" she asked, and I began to smile widely because the first thing that came to my mind was Jaxsyn. He was something new in my life that was bringing me happiness at the moment.

"Uhm, nothing really."

"Yeah, don't lie to me. How are you holding up?" she asked.

"I'm good," I replied.

"That's good..." she trailed off. "Soooo..." she continued.

"Ok. Ok. You busted me. Soo there's this guy." I twirled a piece of my hair in my hand as I thought about Jaxsyn. The way that he was starting to focus on me and the way that he was making my body feel, was just. Oh my god.. it was just... speechless.

"A guy!" she squealed. "Where you meet him at, school?" she continued.

"No...He's kind of older than me," I let her know, reminding myself of exactly how much of an age difference it was between the two of us.

"Older?" she escalated her voice. "Oh my god, Kaizlyn. You're dating an older guy." Hearing her sound so shocked, made me burst out laughing.

"Yes. Older, like five years older..." I trailed off after counting the number of years we were apart.

"Oh, you're dating a grown man. Are y'all fucking?" she whispered the last part, and I giggled.

Right when I was getting ready to go into detail about the two of us, there was a knock on the door. "I have to call you back Emma, ok. He's here," I let her know.

"Tell him that your friend Emma said hey, and I miss you Kaizlyn."

"I will. I miss you too and I promise I will call you back and fill you in on everything," I let her know, and we then ended the phone call and I got up and went to the door.

Opening the door, there stood his fine ass in the doorway, flashing me a pearly white smile as he adjusted his fitted hat and pulled his pants up just a little bit.

"You ready to ride out with a nigga?" He stuffed his hands inside of his pocket and I smiled back at him.

"Yes, let me tell my grandma," I told him.

I rushed and put the cordless phone back onto the charger and went to my grandma's room to let her know that I was leaving.

"Hey Grandma, I'm going to see Keisha with Jaxsyn if that is ok."

"Yes baby, and let me know how she is doing. When do you have to go back to work?" She sat up in her bed and ran her hands over her hair.

"I have to work tomorrow and yes ma'am, I will." I walked over to the side of her bed and gave her a hug.

"You coming home tonight?" She raised her eyebrow up at me as she questioned me.

"Ughh…"

"Ughh…you need to be bringing yo' butt home because you are not grown, and the only reason why I'm letting you get away with so much when it comes to that man is because I have watched him grow up since he was a little boy. Don't think I allow this type of stuff," she informed me, and I nodded.

"Yes ma'am."

"Alright baby, I'll see you later."

"Ok. Bye Grandma."

"Took you long enough." Jaxsyn stood at the bottom of the steps with his phone to his ear as I left out of the front door and made sure to lock it behind me. I didn't want to just leave the door unlocked. Especially after that weird ass man had come by. The man that my grandma had yet to tell me more information about.

"I'm sorry, my grandma was giving me one of those long speeches." I playfully rolled my eyes.

Jaxsyn chuckled, grabbed my hand and we headed to his car. He opened the door for me and I got inside. The inside of his car smelled just like his cologne.

I watched through the window as Jaxsyn walked smoothly around the car, right as his grandpa was coming out of the house.

"Boy, I know you not on my side of town and not coming inside to speak to your people," I heard him yell as he waved in Jaxsyn's direction.

Jaxsyn turned around and headed over to where his grandpa stood. I could no longer hear their conversation but I could tell from the way the two of them interacted and even laughed that they were most likely joking around. Jaxsyn then went inside of his grandma's house and in less than five minutes, he was back out and rushing over to the car.

"I'm sorry about that." He sat down in the car, adjusted his chains around his neck and started the car.

"It's ok," I let him know as he looked down at his phone, sighed and ignored whoever was calling him.

"I got something for you." He reached to the back of the car and pulled out a bag.

My heart began to race and I began to smile from ear to ear. It had been so long since I had received a gift.

"What is it?" I questioned.

"Girl, open it and see." He smirked.

Opening the pretty pink bag and pulling out the white and silver paper, my eyes widened and my mouth dropped. I wanted to squeal loudly, jump over into his lap and rain kisses on him, but I knew that would cause us to end up in a ditch.

"You didn't." I pulled the iPhone Xr out of the bag and opened the box that held the phone.

"Yeah, I had to. I can't be having you around here without a phone. I need to be able to get in contact with yo' ass at all times. I also want to be receiving some freak nasty pictures from yo' ass when you at work and shit." He ran his tongue across his bottom lip then placed his hand on my thigh.

Bashfully, I shook my head and began to open the box. I couldn't hide the smile that was on my face. I was smiling so hard that my cheeks were beginning to hurt. But I couldn't stop, I was just so freaking happy to have a phone. To be able to connect with the world, finally.

"So, you like?" He looked over at me out the corner of his eyes as I powered the phone on just to see that it had already been set up.

"I love it." I could no longer contain myself. I leaned over and planted a kiss on his cheek and went to sit back down, but he grabbed me.

"Nah, come here."

"What?" I giggled.

"Come here. I'm a grown ass man. What kind of kiss was that?" He curled his lip up.

Leaning back over, I kissed his lips and he forcefully stuck his tongue into my mouth. While he drove, he continued to deepen the kiss while trying to watch the road.

"Thank you." I pulled his lip in between my teeth, bit down then sucked on it.

"Shit, you're welcome. Do that shit again though," his freaky as said, and I kissed him one more time. This time, I sucked on his lip a little longer, then let my tongue glide across his bottom lip before I went and had a seat.

"Fuck Kaizlyn, now I want to fuck you." He looked over at me with hooded eyes as he bit down on his lip.

"We have all day for that. I want to go see your sister first," I let him know, as I began to play around with the phone.

I was so excited to have one and I couldn't wait to log back into all of my social media accounts and see what all I had missed with the people I used to go to school with.

"Bet. But when I get you to my house, we not doing no talk. None whatsoever." He winked and I blushed.

The rest of the ride to the hospital was silent. I was so busy playing with the new phone that I got, that I wasn't even paying attention to nothing surrounding me.

"Damn, we here." He tapped me, and I looked up at him. That was my first time looking up from my phone since he gave it to me.

"I hope me getting you this phone isn't going to get you into trouble." He looked at me sternly and I laughed.

"Oh my god, no…" I pushed him. "I was just trying to download all the apps that I would need and sign into my old accounts," I let him know.

"Don't get beat up Kaizlyn," he said in a deep, serious tone, and I then realized that he was no longer playing. He was serious as fuck.

"What could I possibly do to get beat up?" I asked him, confused.

He had just given me the phone and he was already making threats.

"Like I said." He picked his phone up and ignored another call.

"I think you're the one who is going to be the one getting beat up." I tried to look closer into his phone but he quickly stuffed it into his pocket.

I wasn't stupid, and the fact that he was trying to threaten me when it was obvious that he was the one hiding something pissed me off.

I quickly got out of the car. Even though I didn't know what room number Keisha was in, I slammed his door and headed inside of the hospital. Once inside, I didn't know where to go, so I stood in the waiting area, with my arms crossed, as I waited for Jaxsyn to bring his ass inside.

"Oh, I thought you knew where you were going." He chuckled and it only made me madder.

"Whatever Jaxsyn, can we just sign in or whatever we have to do so I can go see your sister. I don't want to sit here and play these games with you," I let him know.

Rubbing his hand across his chin, he looked me up and down, shook his head and didn't say anything. Not a single word. Instead, he walked off and I was left to follow him, assuming that we were on our way to his sister's room.

Twisting around a corner, Jaxsyn stopped in front of the women's bathroom and yanked me inside, not even knowing if somebody was in there.

"What are you doing Jaxsyn?" I squealed, relieved that nobody else was in the bathroom.

"I'm about to teach you a lesson." He pulled me down to the last stall that was big enough to fit about three to four people.

He locked the door behind us, pushed me up against the wall and pulled my pants down forcefully.

"Jaxsyn, what are you doing? We supposed to be on our way up to see your sister," I let him know, but he ignored me.

He forcefully turned my head in the opposite direction. I could hear him undoing his pants and before I could plead for him not to fuck me in a damn hospital bathroom, his dick was trying to enter me.

"Jax... syn..." I whined out his name as he stuffed his dick up inside of me.

The way he filled me, it caused me to gasp and for the scream that I wanted to release to get stuck in my throat.

"Oh, my fucking... god," I screamed out as he rammed his big dick off inside of me, causing my legs to feel weak like a newborn horse.

"Nah, don't call him," he stated as he placed his hands on my waist.

"Say my name. What's my name?"

"Jaxsyn...it's Jaxsyn," I cooed out as my eyes began to roll to the back of my head.

He was delivering straight dick to me and I didn't know if it was because this was all new to me, but I was so turned on.

"Are you going to be storming off mad at me again?" He slapped me on the ass and shoved his dick deep into me.

"Ahh. Ughh..." was the only thing that I could get to escape my mouth.

"Nah. Talk to me, baby." He pulled his dick out of me, bent down and took my pants off even more.

He picked me up as if I was as light as a feather, and I wrapped my legs around him and he entered me.

With his left hand around my neck and his other on the wall for support, he fucked me. He fucked me so good that I wanted to cry out. With my hand wrapped around his neck, I was able to bounce up and down on his dick as I flew my head back. Ecstasy took over my body. The way that Jaxsyn was fucking me right now was driving me crazy. He had my nose wide open.

"Nah, talk to me baby. Are you going to act like that again?" He now had his hands on each side of me as he brought me down aggressively onto his dick.

"Ahh baby..." I screamed so loudly that I knew I alerted a doctor.

"Nah, that's not what I want to hear. I'm going to keep making you take all this dick until you tell me what I want to hear," he whispered into my ear then he bit me on my shoulder.

"No, I'm not going to act like that. Oh my... I not going to act like that," I whimpered as he fucked me so good.

"Good girl, now cum on this dick," he demanded and as if his words were the magical words that I needed to hear to release the flood gates, I rained down on his dick.

"Shit," he moaned as his dick got harder. Seconds later, it began to thump inside of me and then I could feel his warm fluids emptied inside of me.

Lowering me to the ground, I had to hold onto the wall in order for me not to collapse to the ground. He always did that to me when he fucked me. Made me feel weak.

We were both out of breath as we put our clothes on and left out of the bathroom like we hadn't just been in there fucking.

The whole walk to his sister's room, I could feel wetness seeping out of me and that's when I began to panic. I wasn't going to say anything right now but when we left, I was going to let him know that I wasn't on birth control and I was too young to be trying to have kids.

When we finally entered his sister's room, I went over to the sink in her bathroom and washed my hands before I touched her.

The way she laid in the bed, she looked so peaceful and as if nothing was wrong with her.

"Hey Keisha." I grabbed her hand. As I stood there talking to her, Jaxsyn was further in the back just staring at the two of us. I could tell that seeing his sister like this brought him pain, and I felt horrible.

I flashed him a smile and he gave me a simple head nod. I then directed my attention back to Keisha, as I prayed for her and talked to her. I wasn't sure if she could hear me or not, but that was ok.

Jaxsyn

atching Kaizlyn talk to my sister and her not being able to respond to her was like the worst shit that I had ever seen. Like damn, why did God have to fuck with a nigga like this? Why, out of all the people he could have had laying up in this damn hospital bed, it had to be my sister?

Shit, he could have had my mother up in this bitch because she was well overdue for her karma. Speaking of, I had been debating on if I wanted to call her and let her know that her only daughter was laid up in the hospital bed. I hadn't heard from her, but I was debating with myself on if I should ride over there and let her know. Just to see how she would react and what she would say.

"Hey baby, you ready?" Kaizlyn walked over to me, grabbed my hand and laid her head against my arm.

"Yeah, hold up really quick." I walked over to Keisha with Kaizlyn still holding on to my hand.

I leaned forward and kissed my sister on her forehead. I knew that if she was awake she would have cursed me out.

"You think your mother might want to know about this?" Kaizlyn whispered over in my ear, and I looked at her upside her head.

It was like she was reading my mind or some shit, and I just took that as a sign to see where exactly my mother's head was at after all these years.

"I was thinking about going over there. I haven't really been over there since we were kids," I let her know.

Kaizlyn squeezed my hand tighter and looked up at me. "I'll go over there with you babe. I think she should know and however she handles it, will let you know how you should handle her."

The words Kaizlyn spoke were real as fuck. She was right though. All I could do was try and if my mother was still on the same bullshit, then fuck it. The only thing I could do was see where her head was at and hope that I didn't have to unleash on her.

"Aite bet," I replied.

I looked back at my sister once more. I leaned down and whispered in her ear, "I love you and you'll get through this."

I closed my eyes, prayed to God, even though I questioned his way of doing things, then popped my eyes back open and began to head for the door. Kaizlyn was now tucked up underneath my arm as we headed for the elevator.

Once reaching the elevator, I pressed the number one and as I waited for the elevator to open, I looked at Kaizlyn.

"What?" She giggled.

"Nothing. I'm glad I fucked some act right into yo' ass," I joked with her.

I didn't really have time to process the fact that her ass let me fuck her in the bathroom at the hospital. I mean, it wasn't like she had a choice. I needed to fix that damn attitude for her.

"Oh my god, Jaxsyn." She blushed and buried her face against my chest.

"Nah, don't be trying to act shy now. You weren't acting like that when you were letting me beat that…" I stopped talking because when the elevator door opened, rage filled my body and I was ready to knock this nigga out again.

My body had tensed up and I was now breathing heavy as the person that was on my hit list stared me in my eyes.

"Jaxsyn, here is not the place to do whatever you are thinking about doing." Kaizlyn placed her hand on my chest and even though I heard her, that didn't mean I was listening.

"Jaxsyn, do you hear me?" Kaizlyn pulled on my shirt then stepped in front of me.

"Matter fact, let's take the steps." She tried pulling me, but I didn't budge. I stood there as if my feet were glued to the tile floor.

Smirking, I decided that she was right. "Fuck this nigga. If he knows what's best for him, he better not say shit." I mugged the fuck out of Whoodie. I wanted him to step so that I could knock his fool ass out.

I knew that I couldn't cause a big ass scene like I had done the last time. Even though I didn't give a fuck, I just couldn't afford to be in jail while my sister was laid up in the hospital.

Matter fact, why the fuck was he here? I knew mothafuckin' well he wasn't up here trying to see her. Rage filled me and I pounced on him. Kaizlyn was now inside the elevator behind me, begging me not to do nothing stupid.

"I know yo' ass better not be trying to see my fucking sister." I hemmed him up by his shirt.

"Nigga fuck you," he spat back, and I punched his ass dead in the face.

I swear to God, this nigga was weak and he was making shit way too easy for me.

"Nigga I swear on yo' bitch ass mama, that I would kill you and sleep nicely at night. The only thing saving you is…" I paused and thought for a second. "Nothing!" My jaw clenched and my hands were now around his neck.

"I ain't here to see your fucking sister…" he was struggling to get his words out.

"My cousin is up here," he finished.

"Let him go Jaxsyn. You have bigger shit to worry about right now." She was pulling on my shirt.

"Kaizlyn, let me handle this," I raised my voice at her.

I could feel her grip on my shirt loosening and then the elevator door opened.

"You're so stupid Jaxsyn," she said lowly then took off out of the elevator.

Exhaling, I looked him up and down. I dropped his fool ass to the floor and winked at him before using my finger as if it was gun and pointed at him.

"Pow!" I mouthed before I rushed out of the elevator trying to search for Kaizlyn.

I had thought that I fucked her good enough and I wouldn't have to worry about her nasty attitude, but I guess I was wrong. I figured I was going to have to attempt to teach her ass again. She honestly had no reason to be mad. None whatsoever. What I had going on with that nigga was none of her business, and she should have just stayed in her place.

Bursting outside of the automatic doors, I looked to my left and right in search for Kaizlyn. I didn't see her, so I continued walking to my car. When I made it to my car, she wasn't there standing by it.

"What the fuck," I breathed out as I placed my hands on top of my head.

I turned around in a complete circle and headed back inside of the hospital. I was puzzled as to where she could have taken her lil' ass that damn fast.

I walked over farther into the waiting room area and there she was, sitting in a chair in the corner of the room.

Sighing, I looked over at her and she turned her head and began to look outside of the window.

Fuck man, I hissed to myself as I ran my hands down my face and walked over to her. Sitting down in the seat beside her, I grabbed her hand and she snatched it back.

"What is your problem yo?" I asked her, and she rolled her eyes in my face.

"Look Kaizlyn, talk to me or get left here," I told her.

"Bye," she spat, and I had to take a deep breath.

"So you don't want to talk about it?"

"No. For what? It's not like you are going to try to listen to me. It's obvious you do what you want," she sassed.

"Look, I'm all ears. Talk to me." I grabbed her hand back and this time, she didn't snatch it back from me.

Kaizlyn inhaled then exhaled before she began to talk. "I just feel like life is too short to be dwelling on that shit with Whoodie. At least not right now. You got a sister that's up there laying in a bed, in a coma, and you tell me you worried about him? You need to be worried about her and her only right now," Kaizlyn expressed.

Fuck, she was right yet again. I hated to admit that shit, but she was. I shouldn't be worried about that nigga but guess what, I was. I wanted to fucking murk his ass and when the time came, I was. Period. But for the sake of my feelings for Kaizlyn, I was going to act like I was listening and agreed.

"Alright. I'll let it go…"

"No, for real. Seriously." She pouted and pulled her hand away from me.

"I'm serious. What more do you want me to say?" I asked her because damn, what else did she want me to say or do in order for her to believe me?

"Alright, Jaxsyn." She side-eyed me as she got up from the seat.

She began walking away and I just watched, the way her hips swayed from side to side, made my mouth begin to water. I wanted to bend her ass over again and let her know that I did what the fuck I wanted when I wanted, and that I was going to blow Whoodie's brains out but for now, I was going to let her think that her young ass was running the show.

"Are you going to sit there and watch me or are you going to get up?" She turned around and asked as she tapped her foot against the tile floor.

Her question caused the two to three people that were waiting to be seen, to turn their attention on us.

Shaking my head, I walked over to where she stood, grabbed her hand and we walked out of the doors.

"Did you see me when I first ran past there?" I asked her on our way to the car.

"Yes," she stated.

"Why you didn't say nothing?"

"For what? I was pissed at you," she let me know, then she started giggling. "Yo' ass was on a mission to find me, huh?" She burst out laughing loudly.

"Fuck you." I playfully nudged her head.

She was dying laughing and I couldn't help but to laugh too because she was right. I was trying to find her mad ass.

Hitting the unlock button, we got in the car and headed to my mother's house.

* * *

YES, I had rode by here plenty of times too many. Even though I had said fuck my mother and expressed how much I disliked her, I couldn't fight those random urges to ride by the house that I held so many bad memories in. It was like a constant reminder on why I shouldn't forgive her.

Taking a deep breath, I wasn't one that was scared of much but sitting outside of this house caused my heart to race just a little bit. I didn't know why, but the thought of seeing my mother's face just didn't seem to settle in my stomach. Also, the hate that I had for the nigga that she was lying next to, was damn near the same hate I had for the nigga my sister decided to fuck with it.

"You ok?" Kaizlyn reached over and placed her hand over mine that was currently gripping the steering wheel.

"Yeah. Yeah." I shook my head because I had been in a complete daze.

"You ready?" she squeezed my hand.

"As ready as I'll ever be," I told her, and opened my door and got out.

Walking up to the front door with Kaizlyn right next to me, I didn't know why, but I felt like I was walking into a damn jailhouse, getting ready to turn myself in. That's the feeling I got from standing in front of my mother's door.

"Knock." She nudged me and I brought my hand up to knock, but the door flung open and there she stood. My mother. She looked way different than what I remembered but nonetheless, she was still beautiful as ever.

Her chocolate skin shined as the sun hit it and she didn't look how I would have ever imagined her to look. She looked better, she looked healthy and she looked like she had been doing better than I could have ever imagined her to, due to the fact that she was living with a man that would put his hands on her.

"Hey," I dryly said.

No words came out of my mother's mouth; instead, her hands shook and tears started to cascade out of eyes.

The fuck she crying for? I pondered. What was her reason? She had made her decision years ago but now she wanted to cry.

Fuck, I thought.

"Man, I only came over here to tell you that your only daughter is in the hospital, in a coma."

My words must have hit her like a bullet to the heart because the color in her face washed away and she had to hold on to the door for balance. Her knees began to buckle and she was on her way down to the ground.

"Help her," Kaizlyn said and reluctantly, I did.

Helping her inside of her home, we walked over to the couch and I sat her down as her body shook.

"Is she ok?" Her voice trembled as she looked at me with low, red eyes.

"I mean, she's in a coma Ma," I stated, because I didn't know if she was going to be ok. All that I could do was let it play out and pray that she woke up from it.

"Fuck," she screamed as her body just began to shake. She was pulling at her hair and scratching and clawing at her face and skin.

"Chill yo." I grabbed her up into my arms and that only made her break down and cry even harder.

"I'm so sorry Jaxsyn. I'm so sorry…"

As I held my mother, I looked at Kaizlyn whose eyes were big ass the fucking moon. Her mouth was wide open and her eyes were a little misty.

"Please forgive me?" My mother dropped to her knees, her hands balled up together as she pleaded for my forgiveness.

I shook my head because I didn't know. I didn't think that I had it in me to forgive her. That was not why I came over here. All I wanted to do was let her know about her daughter then leave. I wasn't looking to rekindle anything. Not a damn thing.

"Jaxsyn," Kaizlyn called my name which caused me to look in her direction.

Trying to say something to me, without really saying a word, she raised her eyebrows and nodded for me to say something, but I wasn't ready. I didn't have anything to say to the woman that had chosen her fucking abusive ass man over her kids.

"Man, fuck this." I walked away from my mother and she fell to the floor and just laid there. She laid there and continued to cry her eyes out.

I walked out of the house and was headed to my car to leave. I couldn't do this shit. I was a man and faced most shit, but this right here was something that I guess I wasn't ready to face.

"Jaxsyn, stop. Stop," I heard Kaizlyn calling out behind me, but I ignored her. If she didn't want me to leave her ass, she had better get in the car so that we could go.

"Jaxsyn," she yelled so loudly that I didn't even know that her voice could escalate that damn high.

Stopping midway in my stride, I turned around and looked at her. My face didn't wear an expression.

"You only have one mother and she could die tomorrow and you will be filled with regret," she expressed, but I wasn't feeling where she was coming from.

"Nah." I shook my head.

"Yes." She nodded back at me. "Yes, you will. I know you will. Listen to me. Listen to someone who has lost their mother and has to deal with that shit every day. Every day I am left to wonder if my mother would still be alive if I would have just not left out that room when I found her on the floor after being hit by the man that supposedly loved her. Wondering if I would have been more adamant about her taking me to school instead of him. Maybe that one little thing would have her in my life right now, but it doesn't. You have time. Don't take it for granted. I wish that my mother was still here. I would forgive her a thousand and one times for leaving me here in this fucked up world without her." Kaizlyn now had tears in her eyes as she expressed to me her feelings.

Real nigga shit, that shit had pulled at my damn heart. Yet again, she was speaking knowledge to me. I felt where she was coming from and I actually agreed with the shit that she was saying.

Without even saying a word, I walked up to her and wrapped my arms around her. I held her so tightly as she wrapped her arms around me too and buried her head into my chest.

"I feel you ma and I agree with you," I told her, and she lifted her head to look up at me.

"Good, now go in there and forgive her. Hug her too." She gave me a smile even though I knew that she was hurting inside.

"I got you." I smiled back as I leaned down and placed a kiss on her soft lips.

After the kiss, we pulled apart and I wiped her tears away before planting another kiss onto her lips. Kaizlyn was young but every day she was teaching a nigga like me something. She was hitting me with knowledge and making me aware of shit that I normally wouldn't give two fucks about.

Grabbing her hand, we walked back into my mom's house so that we could have a talk and maybe even get a better understanding about shit.

Kaizlyn

*W*atching Jaxsyn interact with his mom right now was bringing me a different kind of feeling. Knowing that he was willing to listen to little ole me and actually take my advice had my damn heart beating hard.

But I was only telling him the real deal. Like he still had a chance to love on his mom, but yet he wanted to be mad about some shit that happened years ago.

"I'm so glad that we talked about all of this and like I've said a million times, I'm sorry. I wish that I knew what I know now back then, because I would have been a better mom to you and your sister." She held Jaxsyn's hands in her hand as she spoke to him.

I could see it in her eyes that she was sorry and that she wasn't playing games, but Jaxsyn was still standoffish but he was open to it. He wasn't being an asshole and he was willing to take the extra step in rekindling their mother and son relationship.

"It's cool Ma. You still have time, but don't fuck up this go-round," Jaxsyn stated, and I had to clear my throat.

Never in a million years would I have cursed around my mom. She would have backhanded me and sent me to meet my maker.

"Respect boy." She tilted her head to the side and looked at him.

"Oh yeah. My bad." He chuckled.

"I'm glad you got rid of that hoe ass nigga." Jaxsyn looked around the house.

"Yeah, me too. I hated I waited so long to do it. It took me calling the laws in order for me to do it, but he was sentenced to three years. He got about three months to go," she spoke as her voice cracked.

"What did he do to you?" I butted in, because I wanted to know.

Standing to her feet, she turned around and raised her shirt. She spun around in a complete circle and from the top of her back all around to the center of her stomach was a long as cut as if he was trying to skin her ass.

I covered my mouth and gasped because I knew that it had to be painful. Jaxsyn sat there as his jaws tightened and his temples began to thump.

"Damn Ma." He shook his head and stood up.

This time, he was the one to bring her in for a hug and again, she began to cry. The whole sight and situation was just too much. My emotions were on ten.

"It's ok. I learned from it. I just hope he did too and doesn't try to step back over here." She gulped.

"Don't worry about that. I got you, but look Mom, I got to jet. I still got some shit to handle. My plans were never to be over here this long." Jaxsyn chuckled. "I'll be back over here to pick you up to see Keisha or you can just go by yourself. Take my number," he told his mom, and she nodded her head then scurried to her purse that was upstairs in her room.

When she came back downstairs, she had a pen and piece of paper ready to write his number down. I could see that she really wanted to get back close with her son, and even her daughter.

Jaxsyn gave her his number and then we said our goodbyes.

"Next time I meet you, it won't be such an emotional moment," she yelled at me as she waved from the door.

Laughing, I waved back and agreed. We didn't even have a chance to even meet or talk about who I was to her son because there was a bigger problem that needed to be solved, and I was glad that I was there to help the both of them because who knows where it would have gone if I wasn't there with his ass.

"Thank you for being here with me today." He paused. "You have no idea how hard this shit was for me. I'm real enough to say that if it had not been for you, I would still be holding that heavy ass weight on my shoulder. I feel way better. Now all I need is for my sister to wake up, so we can get this damn party started." He tried to sound cheerful but his mood totally didn't match the way his words came out.

"You're welcome and she's going to wake up. Just trust God." I beamed and then I leaned over and kissed him.

I don't know what came over Jaxsyn but in one swift movement, he pushed his seat back, grabbed me and I was now in his lap.

"Kaizlyn..." he mumbled my name lowly as he looked up at me with hooded eyes.

He licked his lips as his hands rested on my ass. He firmly gripped it as I licked my lips also and looked into his eyes.

"What..." I dragged and I batted my eyelashes and tried my hardest not to show all thirty-two of my teeth.

Sitting in Jaxsyn's lap right now as I felt his dick get hard had my damn head spinning. The way he was looking at me had me wanting to see exactly how fun car sex was. I mean, back at my old school and even in the group home, I would hear the girls talking about how fun car sex was but never had I really experienced it.

When I was with Melo, we would just sneak and do it at his house. We would touch and feel on each other in his car, but that was about it.

"Why the fuck you so fucking dope yo?" He chuckled.

"I don't know." I shrugged. "I'm just me."

"Well, I like you. A lot." He smirked and I had to lay my head down his shoulder to hide the big ass grin that was on my face.

As I rested my head on his shoulder, he caressed my ass cheeks and I began to kiss and suck on his neck. I knew that he was loving it because his body relaxed and his grip on my ass got firmer and his dick got harder. Jaxsyn even let out a light moan and that made me wet. To know that I was turning him on, turned me on.

"Damn..." he let out as he leaned his head over more to the left, giving me more room to suck on his neck.

I was now planting soft kissing along his neck as I guided my lips up to his earlobe then ran my tongue against his outer ear.

"We gon' fuck right here if you don't stop this shit." He began to hump up and down and I could feel his hard dick pressed against my center which made me want to fuck him. Not here in front of his mother's house, but I definitely wanted to fuck him in the car.

"What if I want to fuck you right now. In yo' car." I tried my best to sound as sexy as I could as I whispered in his ear then bit down on his ear.

"Fuck this shit." He lifted me up and pulled his dick out.

"Jaxsyn, no, not in front of your mama's house." I was shocked that he was really about that life. Yeah, I wanted to fuck him but damn, not in an area where we could get caught.

"Nah, nah baby. You were talking that hot shit in my ear and now you have to handle him." He looked up at me as he stroked his dick.

"But…" I tried to reason with him but he wasn't having it.

"No buts. Handle this shit for yo' nigga." His fine ass bit down on his lip and looked at me with those deep brown eyes, and it was like I couldn't say no. Something took over me and I was now pulling down my pants and climbing on top of his hard dick.

"Yes, handle that shit." He bit down on his lip, grabbed both of my ass cheeks and help me bounce on his dick.

"Are we going to get caught?" I questioned as I looked around. I didn't think that I would be this damn paranoid when I did this shit.

"I want you to focus on me and this nut I want you to bust all over my dick," Jaxsyn spoke as he leaned in and kissed me on my neck.

Throwing my head back, I allowed Jaxsyn to guide me up and down his dick at the speed that he wanted.

The way that his dick filled my pussy up only made me wetter and hornier. The way that he was caressing my ass cheeks while delivering deep strokes had me speechless. He had my whole body tingling. He was an expert with this shit and I was slowly learning.

"How this dick feel?" he asked me, and if he couldn't tell by the way that my face was frowned up and the way that my pussy was gushing all on his dick, if he couldn't use those clues, then I didn't know what to tell him because no words were coming out.

"I said how does it feel?" He slammed me down on his dick and all I could do was scream out.

"Ahh… fuck. It feels. It feels. Oh my." I tried to answer his question, but the sensation and pleasure from his deep strokes had my mind so damn gone.

"Talk to me, baby. I like when you talk to me. Tell me how Daddy dick feel?" he asked again as he bit down on his lip again.

I didn't know what it was about him biting down on his juicy, pink lips and showing off those perfect teeth that turned me on, but it did.

"It feels so good. Too good," I expressed as I placed my hands on his shoulders and began to pick up speed. I was now in control of how fast I wanted to go on his dick.

"You feel good too. Too fucking good, shit. Damn Kaizlyn, slow down," he told me, but I wasn't listening.

I was in a whole different element as I continued to bounce down on his big ass dick, causing my juices to splatter and our skins to smack together.

The windows in the car were getting foggy and it was getting hot as fuck, but I didn't care. My nut was right there and I could feel it deep in my stomach. I knew that when it came that I was going to lose it.

"Jaxsyn... yo' dick be feeling so good," I hollered as I rode his dick in car. "And I'm about to... Ahhh!"

"Yes... nut all on that dick," he said, and that's exactly what I did.

My breathing stopped, my legs felt numb, my stomach ached and my pussy throbbed as I released all on his dick just like he had demanded me to.

"Fuckkkk." Jaxsyn bit down on his lips so that he wouldn't get too loud, and then I felt his warm seeds fill me up.

"Oh my god." I leaned back on the steering wheel which caused the horn to blow, reminding me that we were in the car.

Panicking, I looked around and was so happy to see that nobody was around. I quickly got off of his lap and got in the passenger seat as I pulled up my pants.

"Yo' ass lowkey a freak." He looked at me as he stuffed his dick back into his pants and started the car.

I was happy to feel some cool air blow on me because me and him had just caused the car to get hot and steamy.

"No, I'm not." I laughed.

"Yeah, ok. You'll see." He winked at me and drove off.

I just sat there in the passenger seat, still feeling like his dick was inside of me by the way my pussy throbbed and leaked not only my juices but his nut.

"Jaxsyn," I called his name after riding in silence for about ten minutes.

I had been trying to think about how I wanted to say what I was about to say to him. The way that he was nutting in me, he was going to have me pregnant before I even graduated high school and got the chance to go off to college, and that was not something that I was picturing in my future right now.

"We need to talk." I bit down on my knuckle as I waited for him to say something.

"Well talk… talk to me baby," he stated in a calm tone.

"I'm not on birth control and I don't want no babies right now. So can we go get a plan b or something?" I expressed then held my breath as I waited for him to say something.

Silence filled the car and I began to worry. Like what in the world was he over there thinking about? He should have responded quickly to that shit; it wasn't something that he needed to think about. All he needed to say was, ok babe, I'll stop and get you one.

"You don't even know if you're pregnant yet."

Exhaling, I turned in my seat. "Jaxsyn, that is the whole point of the pill. To stop the shit before we even have to worry about buying a pregnancy test. Can we please stop and get one?" I was so serious right now. There was no smirk on my face.

"Yeah, there's a CVS by my house," he stated then turned the music up, and we just drove in silence until we pulled up to the CVS.

Jaxsyn parked and pulled his wallet out and was getting ready to hand me the money, but I knew that I couldn't go in there to buy it, at least I didn't think so.

"I can't go in there and get it. I'm not old enough."

"What you mean? So you want me to go get it?" He pointed at himself.

I mean, who else was in the car that could go inside to get it? Not me.

"Yes, Jaxsyn. Did you forget that I am only seventeen? You got to be eighteen to buy it, I'm pretty sure," I told him, and he huffed before he got out of the car as if he was mad, and stormed inside of the store.

About fifteen minutes later, he came outside with a bag. He got in the car and threw the bag in my lap, and I was actually offended.

"Damn, is there a problem?" I asked him as I opened the bag to make sure he had gotten the right shit.

"Yes it is. Had me going in there buying some shit I know nothing about. I had to ask the damn ladies in there. Which ended with them giving my ass a speech and telling me to wrap up so I wouldn't be in here buying this type of shit," he explained, and I actually burst out laughing.

"You mad because they told you the truth?"

"Kaizlyn, leave me alone."

"Oh, so you are mad. You should have gotten some condoms out of there while you were at it," I told him as I held the box with the pill in there that I was going to have to take.

I had never had to do this before, so this was going to be all new to me. I didn't know exactly what it was going to do to my body, but I was more scared of pregnancy than anything, so I was just going to have to pray that I would be ok after I took it.

"Kaizlyn, shut up." Jaxsyn looked at me like I had said the dumbest shit ever, but I was serious about the condom thing. At least until I was able to afford to get on some birth control.

Whoodie

$\mathcal{I}$ wish that I could express the amount of hate that I had for that nigga Jaxsyn. Like, just thinking about him made my soul burn. I just wanted him knocked off this fucking earth.

"Man Dex, when you think we should make that move?" I asked Dex as he sat in the passenger seat rolling up a fat ass blunt.

"Shit, I've been waiting on you to say the word," he stated, and he was right. We had been talking about making the move, but it was me who hadn't said the word. I had to remember that I was the boss and that these niggas were waiting on me to give the go.

"You right. Let's definitely make that move as soon as possible, and you sure that he is going to be there at the time you say?"

"Hell yeah." He nodded as he licked the blunt. "He comes around the same time every Sunday."

"Bet," I let him know, and he nodded his head as he fired up the blunt.

We sat in the car smoking, getting high as fuck when my phone rang. Looking down at it, I saw that it was Chyna's ass and ignored it. I wasn't in the mood to hear her whining and complaints. What I wanted right now was not what she was about to give me. I was stressed out and she wasn't going to do anything but add more stress on me.

"So how that nigga Sims doing?" Dex coughed as he passed the blunt to me.

I inhaled that shit, held it in, then released before I began talking.

"He straight. He healing and shit. He was lucky as fuck though," I explained.

Sims was lucky as fuck because lowkey, that nigga could have died. I guess it was just not his time yet.

"That's what's up. I'm glad that nigga made it up out that shit. Real talk." He bobbed his head.

"Hell yeah," I agreed.

I then hit the blunt one more time and passed it. We sat in the car for about thirty more minutes before my phone rang again.

"This hoe," I huffed before I even picked it up.

Dex chuckled but when I read over whose name flashed across my screen, my dick jumped.

"Wait a minute, it's this hoe..." I smiled as I slid my finger across the screen and answered.

"What's up witcha baby?" I picked my cup up that was filled with liquor and took a sip from it.

"Nothing, trying to see you tonight that is all."

"Word, so my uncle doesn't have you working tonight?" I questioned.

It was a Saturday night and I knew most likely his club was poppin', which meant her ass should be working and not calling me.

"I requested the night off just for you," she cooed in the phone.

"Oh yeah? But what if I like my bitches to have money?" I played with her mind.

"I get that, don't worry. but tonight I want you," she shot back and I couldn't lie, she was just what the fuck I needed after the day I had. I knew she was going to bust it open, suck a nigga's dick and not once complain, whine or give me a hard time like I knew Chyna would do.

"Bet, you already know where to find me," I replied, and we then hung up the phone.

"Yo' ass a fool with it." Dex laughed.

"You already know what it is." I chuckled and waited until the lil' bitch pulled up.

Finally, Londyn was pulling up to my house after having me wait for about thirty minutes. Dex was already gone after his lil' dip called him to come over or whatever.

I sat in my car and watched as Londyn hopped out of her car. She had on this tight ass one-piece outfit that allowed me to see her pussy print from where I was. Her stomach had a lil' pudge but shit, nowadays all bitches had that. Her ass was fat and she was looking so damn good, that my dick instantly rocked the fuck up.

Getting out of the car, I leaned up against my car and adjust my black bomber jacket.

"Damn, you looking good tonight," she confessed as she stuck her long orange nail into her mouth seductively.

"Thank you ma. So do you," I said, then pulled her ass close to me.

"You ready for this dick?" I asked as I moved my dreads out of my face.

"Are you ready for this pussy?" she shot back.

She was definitely more my speed. These young hoes didn't know to handle me and I saw now that my ass needed me an older woman. Shit, at least just to fuck on.

Londyn grabbed me by my jacket and led me up to my front door. Since the door was already unlocked, she twisted the knob and let us in.

Pushing me up against the wall, not giving me no chance of closing the front door all the way, Londyn dropped down to her knees, unbuckled my pants and pulled my dick out. As she stroked it, making it harder, I moaned out. "Damn, just look at it."

"It's a big mothafucka, I know." I was cocky as fuck but I knew for a fact that I was packing and if any hoe said different, I didn't mind shoving it down her throat to prove my point.

"Yes. Oh my. Yes." Londyn's eyes lit up and I could see her moving her tongue around in her mouth before she shoved my dick in her mouth and went to work.

Londyn was down there bobbing on my dick like she had a point to prove. Like she wanted my young ass to be stuck on her.

Londyn gagged on my dick as she tried to shove it as far as it would go. If she could have literally swallowed the whole thing, she would have. The way that she was massaging my balls and throating my whole dick had me feeling like I was about to have a heart attack or some shit.

"Damn," I hissed as I pulled my dick out of her mouth and moved to the side a little.

I needed a little time to let my nut go down or she was about to have me nutting in under five minutes.

"Why you running?" She crawled over to me as I clutched my chest.

Damn. I licked my lips and just rested against the wall. Fuck it. I was going to bust a nut anyway so there was no point in trying to stop it.

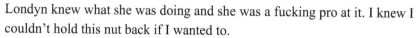

Londyn knew what she was doing and she was a fucking pro at it. I knew I couldn't hold this nut back if I wanted to.

Slipping my dick back into her mouth, she slowly eased it back out and focused on the head of my dick. The most sensitive part. She twirled her tongue around then she began to suck on it as if it was a lollipop. It was like she was trying to see how many fucking sucks, would it take to get to the center because she was going to work and soon she would find out.

"Fuck," I hissed as she shoved my dick back in her mouth as she let it jab the back of her throat.

Spit was everywhere, it felt like I was in some sloppy wet pussy and when sucked her jaws in like a suction cup, I felt like I was now in some tight ass pussy and I was now about to nut.

Pulling out, I beat my dick as she opened her mouth wide open and let me drain all of me in her mouth.

My body was now relaxed and I was ready to go another round, but the sound of my door creeping open caused me to come to my senses real quick.

"Chyna, what the fuck are you doing here?" I was now mad as fuck. She had shown up again at my house unannounced.

"I thought that just maybe…maybe we could have talked it out, but I see now that it's not even an option anymore."

"You fuckin' right. Did you forget what the fuck you had text me? Oh wait, you thought I forgot." I pointed at myself after shoving my dick back in my pants.

I was now walking closer to her. I guess she figured that I forgot or that maybe it wasn't a big deal to me. Oh, but her words did slice my ass like a blade. The fact that she used Jaxsyn, the nigga that I was beefing with, to cut me, I was about to let her ass have it.

"I didn't mean it. I was just mad," she tried to explain.

"Nah, you knew exactly what you were doing and what type of reaction that you were going to get. So that nigga Jaxsyn is going to do what?" I acted as if I was going to hit her duck ass, and she jumped so far back that she almost tripped and fell.

"Whoodie," I heard Londyn call my name, but my focus was on Chyna who just didn't know her place.

"What was that shit you were talking in those texts?"

"I'm sorry Whoodie. I didn't mean it." Just like I knew she would, Chyna's ass was now crying and shit. I hadn't even put my hands on her like I had done the last time. And I wasn't going to have to because what I was about to do, was going to make it loud and clear.

"Londyn, come here," I told her but instead of coming, she stood there confused as fuck.

"Londyn, bring your ass here." I looked at her over my shoulder and she began to walk towards me.

When she reached me, I pulled her close to me, gripped that big ol' booty and kissed her right in Chyna's face. I wanted her to understand something. That she didn't mean shit to me and that she was easy to replace. Also, that I was done with her ass.

"Really Whoodie? Really?" she whined before she lost it.

"I fucking hate I even fucked with you," she yelled as she ran towards me and began swinging on not only me, but Londyn too.

"I fucking hate you. I fucking hate you," she screamed as she continued to try to fight.

Londyn was swinging and my ass had stepped back to let Londyn handle that shit. She was tearing into Chyna's ass. Well, she was until she ended up slipping which caused Chyna to land on top of her.

"You fuckin' bitch." Chyna began to punch Londyn in the face.

Fuck, I quickly made my way over to where the girls were, sprawled out on my floor, and picked Chyna up. Chyna was now kicking, screaming and still swinging. She ended up hitting me in the face, which made me drop her ass. Running back over to Londyn, she kicked her dead in the stomach not once, but three fucking times.

Londyn was now screaming and crying, "I'm pregnant. Get this bitch. I'm pregnant," as she tried to block her stomach.

Hearing her scream that she was pregnant caused the whole room to fall silent, to freeze.

Chyna turned, looked at me and shook her head. She was breathing hard and out of breath. "So you got her pregnant?" she asked.

I didn't know what to say right now because I didn't know shit about the bitch being pregnant, but I knew for sure that it wasn't mine. Me and her had just started fucking around. Even though I was young, I wasn't dumb, and I knew it took a lil' longer to find out if you were pregnant or not.

Stunned by all of it, I couldn't even open my mouth, instead I watched Chyna walk out of my house as if she didn't just walk in this bitch and turn it upside down. She was lucky my people were out of town and I had the house to myself, or it would have been even bigger problems.

If they knew that I had turned their house into a damn hoe house, that Sims had gotten stabbed on their floor and that I had held somebody captive in this bitch, my auntie would have a whole fucking fit, but she wasn't due to be back home until next month, so I was running around this bitch doing whatever I wanted.

Shaking my head, I moved my dreads out of my face and Londyn struggled to get up. I rushed over to her, trying to give her a hand but instead, she slapped my hand away.

"Don't fuckin' touch me. All this shit over your young ass. I haven't had to deal with no shit like this in a minute," she spat as tears streamed down her face and she held onto her stomach.

"How the fuck was I supposed know that you were going to get your ass beat and that you are pregnant?" I mugged her ass.

"It wasn't your fucking business, and I shouldn't even be fighting." She pushed past me and limped out of my house.

Exhaling, I looked around me, made my way to the door and slammed it. Both of them bitches could go. Fuck it.

Chyna

*B*eating my steering wheel as I sped away from Whoodie's place, I couldn't believe that I had lost my damn temper like that. Yes, I could get feisty but for the most part, I felt like I was a lover. I was searching for love in all of the wrong places, or maybe I was too blind when it came to what I really had in front of me, Melo. When we were dating, I never had to worry about being treated bad.

The only altercation we'd ever had was when he broke up with his ex, but that was it. After that, we never had any more problems and here my dumb ass was, chasing behind a guy who meant me no good from the start.

"I fucking hate him." I sniffed as I wiped away the tears and focused on the road. I was never dealing with Whoodie again, and I put that on everything. He was bringing out the worst in me.

Sighing, I turned the music up so loud in my car as I tried to drown out my depressing ass thoughts.

The whole ride to my house, I was crying. I was crying because I should have been smarter. I should have opened my eyes way before it came to me losing my cool and beating a bitch's ass over a nigga that technically never really was mine.

To think that I would have done whatever for him, even if that meant getting in trouble.

Now, a part of me wanted to do some dirty shit and let Jaxsyn know that his sister was raped and beaten with a gun.

I remembered going in the room to check on Keisha and she had been talking in her sleep. She kept mumbling he raped me, he raped me, and then that's when I put two and two together from the conversation that Sims and Whoodie had earlier that day.

Ugh. I shook my head at my own fucked up ways because I should have been a bigger person. I should have never let that go down, but I wanted and I needed to right my wrongs. But sadly, I couldn't do that without throwing Melo under the bus.

Unless… I began to think hard as fuck. I had some shit to put in motion in order to get Whoodie back for playing with my mind and my heart.

Hearing my stomach growl quickly pulled me away from my thoughts.

What's close by? I pondered as I took in my surroundings, trying to think of the closet restaurant near me.

As I drove, the only thing that I spotted open was a freaking IHOP and I swear I was so sick of eating there. Bypassing it, I knew that a Jack-in-the-Box was coming up, so I would just stop there.

Pulling up, I was driving slowly as I made my way to the drive-thru because I was searching in the back seat for my purse. While doing that, a car zoomed around me and cut me off, causing me to stomp on my brakes real hard. I wanted to curse whoever it was out.

"Mothafucka," I said to myself as I laid on the horn and I didn't let up off of it until I felt like they felt my annoyance. On the cool, they had me fucked up and I didn't appreciate their ass cutting in front of me.

As I waited for them to finish ordering their food, I ordered mine and pulled behind the all-black Charger. The music in the car was so loud, that the trunk was rattling. I couldn't see inside because the windows were tinted, but I knew it was a guy.

I slowly crept behind the car and I watched as he stuck his hand out, grabbed his drink and paid for his food. He was also saying something to the lady and she smiled at whatever he was saying.

Rolling my eyes, I assumed whoever he was, he was most definitely a ladies man.

As I waited for them to hurry up and give the guy in front of me his food, I became annoyed when my gas light came on.

Sighing, I guessed I should be thankful that the Jack-in-the-Box was connected to a gas station.

Finally, the guy got his food and I was able to pull forward. My money rested in my lap as I gathered it together, getting ready to pay as the lady repeated my order out to me.

"… your total is. Oh wait, the guy that was just ahead of you paid for your meal," she let me know, and I was confused. Hell, he didn't even know me.

"You sure?" I asked.

"Yes, and he was a cutie too." She winked at me as she handed me my drink and now I wanted to know who in the hell he was.

I actually wanted to tell him thank you.

After getting my food, I pulled around the gas station and parked next to pump six. Grabbing my money to pay for my gas, I noticed the same black Charger parked in front of the store. As I walked up to the store, a part of me wanted to knock on his window so that I could tell him thank you, but I was too scared to.

Bypassing the car, I paid for my gas and headed back out of the store.

"Aye, you can say thank you," the guy rolled his window down and yelled out the car.

I stopped in my tracks and looked back at him. "Thank you."

"No problem, with yo' fine ass." He winked then let his window up, and I blushed as I walked to my car.

Whomever he was, he was fine as fuck. I couldn't take in his whole appearance but what I had observed, I liked what I saw. He had these light brown eyes, thin but pink lips, his skin was a chestnut color and he had braids. Even though I felt like braids were out of style, he looked good with them.

As I thought about the guy that I had just met, I took the nozzle off of the handle as I unscrewed the cap to my gas tank.

Feeling someone behind me, I damn near jumped out of my skin when I saw that it was him.

"Oh my… you can't be running up behind someone like that. I could have stabbed your ass or something," I stated as I continued to breathe hard from the mini heart attack that I'd just had.

He chuckled as he grabbed the nozzle from me and began to pump my gas for me. "I'm not worried about that shit shorty. Try getting shot." He laughed as if that was something normal people said. "And why you out here pumping gas this late by yourself, where is yo nigga at?" he asked as he eyed me up and down.

"Don't have one." I shrugged.

"Word." He turned to me, licked his lips, and I burst out laughing.

Was this his form at getting at me? It was cute or whatever. "You're funny."

"What's funny about me? I don't find shit funny about me. I'm a real ass nigga that do real ass shit. I paid for your food and I'm out here pumping yo' gas for you. So what's funny about that?" he asked me in a serious tone. His facial expression was now cold and he was looking at me with a blank stare, waiting for me to answer his question.

"I didn't mean it like that."

"Well how else did you mean it?" He finished pumping my gas and as he stood in front of me, he pulled his pants up just a little, folded his arms and looked at me as I nibbled on my lip, thinking of the right words to say to him.

"Nothing. Are you done? Can I go now?" I huffed, as I rolled my eyes and folded my arms across my chest.

I didn't know an answer to his question and the best way I knew to avoid a question was just to have a dry ass attitude for no reason. It worked like a charm for the most part.

"Oh, you one of those?" He laughed as he ran his hand down his face then rubbed his hands together.

"What?" I scrunched up my face in confusion. "One of what?"

"Don't worry about it. I know how to fix it." He walked up on me and I backed up against my car.

"Back up, I don't know you like that," I told him.

The closer he got to me, the more I could smell his cologne. Whatever fragrance it was had me closing my eyes as I took it in.

"My name Bjay, by the way. What's yours?" I opened my eyes and he was standing right in front of me.

I blinked a few times as I looked at him. "My name is Chyna."

"Chyna, huh?" He rubbed his chin. "Well look. I'm going to give you my number and I want you to call me as soon as yo' ass hit your front door, and don't try to play me because trust, I'll be seeing you around here again." He pulled his iPhone out of his pocket and handed it to me.

I looked down at his phone then back up at him. I gave him a faint smile then keyed my number and my name into his phone.

"Thank you." He grabbed his phone back and called my number.

My phone began to ring inside of my car.

"Save me as daddy because you'll be calling me that soon." He winked at me and walked off.

Wow, I thought with my mouth wide open. I turned and watched as he walked to his car. I was still in disbelief at what he had just said to me.

Getting in my car, I grabbed my phone and looked over his number. Sighing, I placed my phone down and headed home. I wasn't really worried about a nigga right now because truth be told, I had enough shit on my plate.

When I arrived home, I sat in my car and ate my cold ass food as I scrolled through Facebook and read over the messages that Whoodie had been sending me. He was pissed at me and I didn't even care. I was so over him and the games he wanted to play.

After eating, I got out of the car and went to the front door. Not being surprised by the fact that my mom wasn't home, I unlocked the door and headed straight for my room. I wanted a long, hot shower, and to lay in my bed with the hopes that I could get some peace of mind because right now, I was going through so much.

While I searched for me some clothes, I heard my phone go off. Knowing that it was most likely Whoodie saying even more disrespectful stuff, I sighed before I walked over to pick up my phone.

I sat down on my bed and when I saw that it wasn't Whoodie, I quickly opened the message.

713-879-5484: I know I told yo' ass to text me when you got home. I know it doesn't take that long to get home.

Rolling my eyes but laughing at the same time, I texted him back. Like who did he think he was?

Me: I didn't know I was on a time schedule. Maybe you didn't give me enough time to text you back.

713-879-5484: I gave you all the time you needed. That's strike one. Text me when you wake up in the morning beautiful.

I read over his text, shook my head and simply texted back ok. I could already tell that he was trying to run some shit, and I wasn't having that. Tossing my phone back on my bed, I went and got in the shower.

After I was done with my shower, I was now tucked in my bed, watching TV. I was trying my hardest not to think of Whoodie, but it was so hard. It was like I was hooked on his ass and I hated that shit. I just wanted to forget him. I wanted to go back to my life before I met his ass.

Sighing, I shut my TV off, turned over on my stomach and called Melo. I knew that him lying beside me was the only way I was going to get some good sleep. I hated that I used him for my own personal reasons, but he let me and he never seemed to have a problem with it.

Closing my eyes tightly as his phone rang and rang, I huffed once I reached his voicemail.

Fuck it. I placed my phone under my pillow, closed my eyes tightly and forced myself to go to sleep.

Melo

*S*omehow I found myself back in the same situation that I swore was going to only happen once. I was currently sitting on the edge of the bed, looking down at my phone as Chyna called me. I had to ignore her call because what did it look like me answering and I was in a hotel with her mother.

I thought that I was getting myself out of the situation by fucking her the last time but nope, that only made her have more shit to hold over my head. It was like I was steady giving her ammunition, for her loaded gun.

"Who was that, my daughter?" She looked back at me as she stood in front of the mirror in the hotel room.

Ignoring her, I shook my head because Chyna's mother wasn't right in the head. Yeah, she had some good pussy, but now she was on some me and her type of shit. She was saying how she never had dick so good before and she couldn't picture herself leaving me alone, and that I had no choice but to leave Chyna alone or just deal with the both of us.

That shit had disturbed me and I was on the verge of just going ahead and telling Chyna just so I wouldn't have to keep fucking her.

"Why are you so upset? You don't like the way I suck your dick and fuck you?" She walked in front of me and stepped in between my legs.

She allowed her hands to run up and down my back as she flaunted her nice sized breasts in my face.

"Man, move." I shoved her back. Not in a way that would hurt her. I just needed her to get up out of my face.

"Melo, you act like I made you fuck me. You wanted to." She seductively walked back over to me, unlatched her bra and let it fall the floor.

Now with nothing but a lace thong on, she stood in front of me, grabbing on her breasts and twirling her hips in a seductive manner.

"Melo, I just want to be here for you," she moaned out. She reached for my hand and I pulled back.

"Come on," she began to whine as she climbed in the bed and straddled me.

"I know you don't want me to tell my poor little daughter that you are fucking the shit out of her mom, now do you?" She was now pushing me back onto my back and grinding her hips on top of my dick as if it was inside of her.

Man, this is fucked up, I thought as she grabbed my hand and placed it on her breast. "How long are you going to keep this up?" I asked her, and she paused, bit down on her lip and pondered.

"As long as I want." She laughed, eased off the top of me and fiddled with the string inside of my shorts until she untied it. Once they were loose, she pulled my dick out and stroked it to life.

I hated that my dick would betray my mind. It would do its own thing and come to life for her every time.

"See, he knows what you really want." She beamed.

Mrs. Jade then slid my dick into her mouth, causing me to hiss and close my eyes. I was just going to enjoy this ride because there was no telling her no. Especially if I didn't want her to expose me.

THE LIGHT SNORES of Jade and the numbness of my arm had woken me up. Easing my arm from underneath her, I looked at the time and saw that it was only six twenty in the morning.

Slowly, making my way out of the bed, the feeling of her body moving caused me to pause and be still. Once I saw that she wasn't waking up, I got out of bed and searched for my clothes that were scattered all over the place. Last night, well this morning was such a blur to me. The things that Jade had me doing to her body was one out of this world. The shit she liked was an all new experience for me. From sticking shit in her ass, while I fucked her from the back to her having me place these metal clamps on her nipples. She was into some weird, kinky shit and it was all new to me.

Yes, I had fucked bitches in every position you could imagine but sticking shit in their asses and clamping shit on their nipples was all new to me and strange. But the way that she exploded on my dick had amazed me. It was like Jade's kinky pleasure turned her on in ways that my dick alone could never do. I had to give it to her, her pussy was wet, tight and everything a nigga who wanted her would want. I didn't want her and I had to figure out how in the fuck was I going to get myself out of this situation.

I had finally found my clothes and managed to slip them on without waking her. Now, I was looking around the room in search of my phone. I needed to see if my mom had called me and also to see if Chyna may have hit me up.

What the hell, I thought as I squinted my eyes. My phone was on her side of the bed, underneath her pillow. This bitch was making sure that I couldn't go anywhere unless I wanted to wake her.

Fuck, I exhaled as I paced back and forth with my hands on top of my head. I was trying to get the fuck up out of here.

Sighing, I went back around to my side. I laid back down and wrapped my arm around her. Doing exactly what I thought she would, Jade cuddled up underneath me, giving me access to grab my phone from underneath the pillow. With my phone now in my hand, I now had to figure out what I was going to do in order to get up out of here.

As I laid there, I counted down the seconds, hoping that she would just turn over or get the fuck up and go to the bathroom

God, please help me with this. I promise I'll confess everything. I said a silent prayer to myself and just like that, it was like God answered it. Jade scooted off of my arm, flopped around until she got comfortable again then began to fill the room with her snores.

Excited as fuck, I eased back out of the bed, slipped my feet into my slides, grabbed my keys off of the table and jetted out of the door. I left the door slightly cracked because I didn't want her to hear it shut, then her crazy ass would wake up.

I was damn near sprinting to the elevator. When I reached it, I quickly pressed the number one multiple times hoping that it would speed up the process.

"Come on man," I said out loud as I looked down the hallway, praying that Jade didn't walk out of the room.

Finally, the door opened, and I rushed inside as a black couple got off. I felt like I was running from the fucking cops the way that I was trying to get out of this hotel. As soon as the door dinged, I got off, darted out of the front doors and never looked over my shoulders.

I was now in my car and I felt so relieved, but I knew that it wouldn't last long because as soon as Jade woke up, she would be on her shit. She would be texting me, making threats about telling Chyna. I knew she would also follow through with setting up our next encounter.

Starting my car up, I left out of the parking lot and headed home. While driving, I scanned through my phone, looking for Chyna's thread, only to see that it was deleted.

The fuck? I thought as I continued to scroll, because I knew that Chyna's text messages should have been at the top. I clicked out of my messages, went to my contacts and Chyna's name wasn't even saved.

The fuck did this bitch do? I questioned. She had deleted Chyna's name out of my phone which left me to wonder what else had she done. Had she said something to her?

Frustrated, I squeeze my phone tightly. I squeezed it so tightly that the screen cracked. Tossing the phone onto the floor, I sped home. When I reached my yard, I saw that my mom's car was parked in its usual spot but there was another car beside hers which was my usual spot.

Huffing, due to the fact that I was already aggravated, I just parked my car on the side of the road by our house and got out. Tired and wondering who was in my house, I walked inside of the house and there in the kitchen was my mom, singing, dancing and cooking breakfast.

"Mom, whose car is that?" I asked her, and she stopped dancing. She froze as a blank expression was now on her face.

She looked at me then she looked around, I guess waiting for whoever she had over to appear from around the corner.

"Uhm Melo, let me talk to you," she stuttered.

"About..." I asked her.

"Hey baby, is the breakfast almost done?" a deep voice asked from behind me.

I turned slowly around and the person that was walking into the kitchen and wrapping his arms around my mother threw me for a whole loop. Like, was my mom seriously losing her fucking mind?

She had to be, and there was no way I was going to stand for this shit. This man was a fucking murderer.

Kaizlyn

"**W**hy are you so beautiful?" Jaxsyn asked as he walked up behind me and wrapped his arms around my lower waist.

"My mama and my daddy." I giggled, but Jaxsyn's face went complete stale.

"What is it?" I turned to face him. I placed my hands on his face and looked into his deep brown eyes.

"Nothing." He shook his head then walked away from me.

The blissful feeling that I was feeling after the morning we had, was now turned into me being in my feelings. Like damn, how could somebody just switch like that, for no reason?

"Seriously Jaxsyn, whatever." I rolled my eyes and continued getting ready for work. I didn't have time for his fucked up ass attitude right now. Especially since I didn't do anything to him.

Jaxsyn didn't even respond to what I said; instead, he sat on the edge of the bed. Shaking my head, I finished brushing my hair out then picked up the Plan B box. I was supposed to take this pill last night but I was too scared to. In the back of my mind, I kept asking myself all of these what if questions. I had never taken one of these pills before and I didn't know what it was going to do to my body. I didn't even know if it was going to work.

Spinning the box around in my hand, I opened the box and popped out the tiny pea-size pill and sat it on the tip of my tongue. I bent down towards the sink, cut the water on, and drank it. I swallowed the pill then rinsed my mouth out again to get the nasty taste out of my mouth from the coating of the pill.

As I looked in the mirror, I turned to the side and began to picture myself pregnant. I even poked out my stomach as far as it could go, and I couldn't do anything but laugh.

Hell no. I shook my head at those crazy ass pregnancy thoughts and walked into the bedroom.

"Jaxsyn, I'm ready," I told him.

I then grabbed my purse, my new phone that he had gotten me and walked out of the room. I didn't need him saying anything to me. If that was how he wanted to act then cool. I wasn't about to kiss his ass.

"You ready?" he asked me once he got down the stairs.

Annoyed, I rolled my eyes at him and left out of the front door, with him only a couple of steps behind me. Once we both got in the car, Jaxsyn took in a deep breath then looked at me.

"I'm sorry Kaizlyn, it's just some shit that I know but it's not my place to tell you. I wish that I could because I don't like not being straight up with you on some real shit." He shook his head and now I was confused as fuck.

"What are you talking about?" I turned and asked him.

"You just need to talk to your grandma. That's all," he stated. He then started the car and pulled out of his yard.

My brain was in overdrive. I wanted to know what he was talking about. I knew that me and my grandma were supposed to be having a talk about that guy but we never got around to do it. For one, I had been so far up Jaxsyn's ass that I couldn't even tell you what my grandma's house looked like.

I mean, I enjoyed spending my time with him. I didn't have anyone else but I felt like it was now time for me to go home and chop it up with my grandma. We needed to get down to the bottom of all of the secrets and stuff that she was holding back from.

"I'll have my grandma pick me up tonight when I get off and plus, I have school in the morning anyway," I told him as he pulled up to the front of my job.

I didn't even bother looking up at him as I reached for the door handle to get out. Jaxsyn grabbed me by the arm which caused me to turn and look at him.

"Don't be mad at me. This ain't between us," he stated.

"You right, but the moment you decided to get an attitude about it, you made it about the two of us. I will call you when I go on my break Jaxsyn." I then jerked away from him, threw my purse over my shoulder and walked into work.

The first person to greet me was Mr. Thomas, smiling all hard and shit. I wasn't in the mood to be extra friendly. I just wanted to do my job and pray that the customers didn't get on my nerves.

"Ten more minutes," I whispered as I looked at the time on my register as I scanned the items for the little old lady.

"You're total is $50.42," I told her as I began to bag her things for her.

She smiled at me and pulled out her bank card. Her little old hands shook as she tried to put it inside of the chip e-reader, so I stopped bagging her things and helped her.

"Let me help you." I smiled and walked around and stuck the card inside of the slot.

"There you go." I nodded, as I made my way back around to my area and followed the directions on the screen.

"You can take your card out now," I let her know as I continued to bag her stuff.

Once done, I gave her, her receipt and placed her bags in her basket for her.

"Thank you, sweetie. Have a nice day." She smiled so widely that the wrinkles on her face scrunched up and caused her eyes to close.

"You too." I waved goodbye.

Mr. Thomas was now making his way over to me and when I looked at the screen on the register, I saw that it was now time for me to go on break. I was thankful because my feet were barking and my head was spinning a little. I didn't know if it was because I took that plan b pill or what, but I needed to have a seat as soon as possible.

"You are doing really good," Mr. Thomas stated. He then used his key that was connected to his belt loop and locked my register.

"Thank God." I placed my hand over my heart, relieved.

I didn't think that I was doing a horrible job, but I also knew that I was having a little trouble with the people that would come in with a million damn coupons wanting me to figure out what was free and what they had to pay for. My ass just wanted to throw all that shit in a bag and let them have everything for free. But thankfully, a chick by the name of Niecy helped me.

"Well, you can go on break now. And make sure you come back on time." He playfully nudged me and I laughed and nodded my head.

I was now walking away from the register, excited to go in the break room and sit down and rest my feet until I heard my name being called.

"Kaizlyn," a familiar voice called out and even though a part of me said bitch don't turn around, fuck him, I froze. I was stuck in my stance, scared to turn around and face him.

It had been a while since I'd heard his voice or seen his face, and I didn't know if I was even ready yet.

Inhaling, I turned and there he stood. He hadn't changed much. He still looked exactly how I remembered him too.

"Melo," I said his name out loud, but I said it so softly that I could only hear myself.

"Damn, it's been a minute." He walked over to me and pulled me in for a hug.

Wow, I said to myself. It had been months since I had been wrapped up in his arms. I honestly thought that I left him and all those who stayed on that side of town there, but I guess this world was just too small and no matter how far you thought you were running, you couldn't run away from your past. Especially one that caused you pain.

"Yeah it has." I shook my head as I came back to the reality of everything.

"So what you been up to? And I'm sorry about your loss." He licked his lips and looked me up down.

This nigga. How could you tell me you're sorry about my loss but be checking me out at the same time?

"Thank you and I've been good."

"Yeah, she straight," I heard Jaxsyn's voice, and my eyes got so damn big and my heart stopped.

I don't know why, but I panicked. It wasn't like I was doing something I ain't have no business, but I knew that these types of things never really ended good.

"Damn, is that you?" Melo stepped back and clasped his hands together.

"Yeah, my nigga, is there a problem?" Jaxsyn stepped to Melo and I swear it felt like the whole room was spinning.

"Shit, I was just speaking."

"Now you done!" Jaxsyn's lip curled up and his nose flared out.

He had turned his thug ass ways on one thousand and I knew he was ready to go toe for toe with Melo if need be.

Melo threw his hands up in mock surrender as he backed away from the both of us.

"Nah, I need you to step yo' ass up out of here." Jaxsyn sized Melo up then looked towards the door.

"Jaxsyn." I was finally able to process all of this shit as I grabbed Jaxsyn's arm.

I should have known from the last time, that when he was mad to just stay in my place and wait until he cooled down and prayed that he didn't get himself in trouble, but I guess I didn't learn because just as fast I reached out to grab him, he was jerking away from me, turning to glare at me.

"Please take this outside." Mr. Thomas walked over to where we were standing and told the two guys.

Jaxsyn didn't say shit. Instead, he pulled his pants up and walked towards the doorway, following behind Melo.

Oh my god, I wanted to cry. Why in the hell was Jaxsyn up here at my job showing his naked ass. Like, did he not care?

"Jaxsyn this is my job. Can you please stop." I pulled on him.

"Exactly, this is your job. Not no damn meet and greet. The fuck was this nigga all up in your face for? Do you know him?" He turned and raised his voice at me.

Now the argument was between me and him. Melo was now walking over to the same blue Mustang that I remembered him having when we were together.

"Oh, so you don't hear me?" Jaxsyn barked.

"I hear you Jaxsyn, damn," I shouted as I ran my hands through my hair. "Yes, I know him. He went to my old school..." I paused.

"And what else?" he asked as he looked over his shoulder to check out his surroundings.

"Why the fuck was he so fucking comfortable with being that friendly with you?" He pointed towards Melo's car and I swear I could have melted to the fucking ground.

There was now a crowd outside of the store and Jaxsyn didn't give not one damn fuck about it. I, on the other hand, was so embarrassed. I didn't even think that I would even be able to show my face here ever again.

"He's my ex. Damn, you happy now." I pushed his chest because I was so fucking frustrated.

Tears were now running down my face, and I just wanted to punch him in the chest for showing his ass like that and embarrassing me when it wasn't even nothing like that.

Chuckling, Jaxsyn ran his hand down his face then looked at me up and down. He then shook his head and walked off.

I was left there standing there with tears raining down my face as the cool breeze dried them up, just as fast they were coming down.

I could hear the whispers of the people that were standing around and I swear, I had never felt this type of embarrassment before. This shit was just too much and I swear I was so done with Jaxsyn for the stunt that he had pulled.

Jaxsyn

*J*ust imagine how I felt when I walked in to take my girl out to eat on her lunch break only to see a nigga too cozy up in her fucking face. Yeah, pissed. Nah, pissed wasn't how I felt. I was ready to blow that nigga's head off of his shoulder.

Especially with the way my mental state was set up these day. I was a ticking time bomb and I felt like Kaizlyn didn't understand that. It was like, I had to write the shit down on a piece of paper in order for her to understand it.

Shaking my head, I pulled up to my front yard and parked. I sat in my car a few seconds as I got my damn thoughts together. I was definitely going over to the lil' shop to go and chill with my boys. I needed to drink and light me up a blunt or something. Shit, I might even need to bust a damn nut. My stress levels were at an all-time high right now and I just needed to relax my damn mind.

Fuck that, I needed for my sister to wake the fuck up and make everything around me that much easier.

"Fuck man," I hollered out as I punched the steering wheel causing my horn to blare loudly.

Taking in a few deep breaths, I leaned back and rested my hands on top of my head.

Let me get out this car, I thought as I grabbed my now ringing phone and got out the car. I looked down and I swear, I didn't miss her either. I didn't even feel like dealing with the drama she was about to bring but shit since I was already dealing with fuck ass bullshit, I might as well see what she wanted.

"What Londyn?" I asked, annoyed as I walked up to my front door.

"I lost the baby," she screamed into the phone. She was so loud that I had to pull the phone away from my ear.

"Stop screaming. You what?" I asked again. I had heard her clearly but I needed her to repeat the shit again.

"I lost the baby Jaxsyn." She lowered her voice and sniffled.

I didn't know what she wanted me to say. Truth to it all, I never felt like the baby was mine.

"Why are you calling me though Londyn? The baby wasn't even mine," I stated, and the phone fell completely silent.

"You know what, fuck you Jaxsyn. You fucking bitch," she yelled then she hung up the phone.

Shrugging my shoulders, I set my phone down on the bar and made my way upstairs to my room. I took a shower, changed clothes and was now headed back out the door to go hang out at the shop.

I was now pulling up to the shop and it was like today it was extra packed. I guess a lot of the niggas needed to get out of the house.

Getting out of my car, I didn't know why, but a weird feeling came over me. I had never felt like I needed to carry my gun on me when I was going inside of the shop, but the way my day was going and the weird ass feeling that I had in my gut, I reached under my seat and placed my gun in my lap.

I got out of my car, tucked my gun in the back of my pants and walked inside. When I entered, everybody was doing their normal activity. The tv was on the sports channel, and Mr. Eddie was cutting hair while a few people waited to be next.

My niggas were in the corner playing dice and the crowd was just how it was any other time. Laughs, drinks and just guy talk. It was just what I needed after the day that I had.

"What's good?" I walked over to my niggas and none of them looked up from the dice game.

"Here goes this cheating ass nigga," Bjay joked as he rolled the dice, snapped his fingers and then picked the dice up again.

"Nah, you just ain't got no luck." I chuckled as I walked over to Ace and dabbed him up.

"What's good. Yo' ass been boo'd the fuck up and I ain't heard from yo' ass." Ace kidded with me and I sighed.

"Man fuck her," I stated, and everybody popped their heads up and side-eyed me. Then they all burst out into laughter and started cracking jokes.

"That pussy must got some power." Rell laughed.

"Hell yeah, look at this nigga. 'Man, fuck her,'" Bjay mimicked me, and I had to laugh my damn self.

"Man, y'all get off my boy." Ace laughed. "So, what her young ass do to you to have you up in here in your feelings?" Ace questioned.

"Shit had a nigga smiling all up in her face," I admitted.

"And you snapped because of that?" Ace looked at me as if I had tripped for nothing.

"Hell yeah. Ain't I supposed to? I walked up in her job to take her ass to lunch and she got a nigga in her face. I lost it. Period." I shrugged.

"Man, did you forget that shorty is bad as fuck? You crazy. I would have made that nigga bounce the fuck back but I would have just talked to my shorty. Now she free game. That nigga probably hitting her up on Facebook right now," Ace joked, but my ass didn't feel that fucking joke. It was no akekee, ha-ha for me.

Wasn't shit funny about Kaizlyn getting hit up by another nigga. Which made me pull my phone out and call her. As the phone rang, in walked that same nigga that I was suspect about.

While I waited for Kaizlyn to answer, I nudged Ace to bring it to his attention.

"Hello," Kaizlyn dryly answered her phone.

"Where you at?" I questioned her, never taking my eyes off of the nigga that I was skeptical of.

"I'm at work Jaxsyn. Where else would I be? What do you want?"

"To tell you that I'm sorry and that I am picking you up from work tonight. So, call yo' grandma and let her know," I told her.

"No, I'm good on you."

"What the fuck did I say Kaizlyn?"

"Whatever Jaxsyn," she sassed right before she hung up in my face.

Shaking my head, I chopped it up with Ace about some shit and then before I knew it, I looked down at my Apple watch and saw that it was close to the time that I needed to go pick Kaizlyn up from work.

"Well, I'm out. I got to go pick my girl up from work." I dabbed everybody up.

"Damn, y'all made up that damn fast?" Bjay laughed and so did Ace.

"Nigga mind ya business." I playfully squared up with him and we began to playfully box each other.

As we played around and shit, the nigga that I wasn't too sure about walked out of the shop as he texted away on his phone. See, this was why I had brought my gun with me because I felt like I was going to have to let that hoe loose.

"Well let me go before I be late and shit," I stated as I left out of the shop.

The moment I stepped foot outside, I looked around and didn't see anything out of the ordinary. I made a quick jog to my car and got in. Before starting my car, I pulled my gun from behind me and placed it in my lap.

Pulling away, I drove slowly just so that I could peep everything. I had to make sure that nobody was following behind me.

After driving for about ten minutes, I felt safe enough, so I turned my music up and jammed until the music was interrupted by the ringing of my phone.

"Hello," I answered.

"Hello, is this the brother of La'Keisha King?" I was asked, and I didn't know why, but my heart just began to drop as the worst thoughts began to go through my head.

"What's up? Is my sister good?" I questioned, getting ready to bust an illegal U-turn so that I could head to the hospital.

"Oh. Yes. Yes. Don't panic. I just wanted to let you know that she is awake now. She is asking for you." It was like hearing that shit had made everything that I had gone through today worth it. It was like everything that I was upset about didn't matter anymore.

"Thank you, I'm on my way." I hung up with the doctor as an all-black car pulled up next to me.

It was like I had witnessed this shit too many times and it seemed like everything was moving in slow motion, but all that could be heard now was gunshots.

Pow! Pow! Pow!

Kaizlyn

*L*ooking down at my phone, I knew I should not have called my grandma and told her to not come because Jaxsyn was now twenty minutes late. I was currently sitting outside of my job waiting for him.

Sighing, I tried dialing his number one more time and just like the other twenty calls, it just kept ringing.

A part of me was panicking because I didn't know what could have been wrong. There were so many different things that could be the problem right now and I just wished that he would answer his phone.

Damn. I tucked a piece of hair behind my ear and this time I dialed my grandma's number. Her phone rang and rang and just like Jaxsyn, she didn't pick up either.

What the fuck. I began to get mad because now I was going to be stranded outside of this damn job and I didn't know anybody else who I could call and ask for a ride.

"Hey, you need a ride." Niecy walked out of the store.

She was laughing and talking to Mr. Thomas. They had just finished cleaning the store and counting the cash down.

"Please, if you don't mind." I stood to my feet.

"I don't mind. My car is over here." She pointed to a red Pontiac.

"Alright, bye Mr. Thomas." Niecy waved.

"Bye you guys and Kaizlyn, tell your grandma that I want that meal she promised me," Mr. Thomas joked as he waved us goodbye.

"Ok. I will tell her as soon as I get to the house," I let him know.

I then followed Niecy to her car and we got inside. Once I had a seat in the passenger's seat, I felt a whole bunch of papers underneath my foot. There were empty bottles of water everywhere, food crumbs and even spilled drinks in the cup holder. Her car was a mess and when I looked in the back seat, there were clothes and stuff everywhere.

"Sorry about the mess." She awkwardly looked around her car as if she didn't know that it was a mess already. She even began to try to pick up stuff as if that was going to make a difference.

"It's ok." I gave her a faint smile. I was just happy to be out of the cold and with a way home.

I didn't know why Jaxsyn or my grandma weren't answering their phones. All I could do was pray that nothing was wrong.

"Where do you stay?" Niecy asked as he started up her car and began to drive out of the parking lot.

I gave her my address and she put it into her GPS and we drove in silence.

"Why have I never seen you with Mrs. Daisey before?" she questioned.

"Well, I just moved with her. I just found out that she is my grandma," I stated.

"Oh wow, where were you before this?" she asked, and I huffed.

She was being too nosey and I didn't want to talk about that right now.

"I don't really want to discuss that," I let her know, and she apologized and shook her head.

Finally, we pulled up to my house and I thanked her for the ride. I even offered to pay her gas money when I got my check, but she told me that it was ok and that if I ever needed a ride again, that she would be more than welcome to give me one.

Exhaling after the long day I had, I still couldn't believe Jaxsyn. I couldn't believe that I had seen Melo. I thought that when I saw him that I would feel that pain I felt whenever he broke up with me, but I actually didn't feel shit.

Then the fact that Jaxsyn didn't even care to really hear me out had pissed me off too and when I did hear from his ass, I was going to let him know about himself. Things between me and him just weren't about to be all peaches and cream, especially after the show that he had pulled.

Running my hands through my hair, I tightened my jacket as I ran up the stairs and to the front door. I placed my hand on the doorknob and it was like a strong electric shock shot through my body. Opening the door slowly, my mouth dropped at the sight of the house.

There were pictures slung all off of the wall onto the floor. There was glass everywhere. The pillows to the couch were all on the floor and the vases that once held flowers in them was shattered.

"Grandma," I called out as I closed my eyes and hoped that I wasn't about to have to relive the same thing I had before.

Even though the scenery was different, all of this felt too familiar. Dropping my bags, I walked through the mess that decorated the living room floor as I held my breath, hoping that like last time she was in her room and that nothing was wrong.

"Grandma," I called out again, and I could feel the tears starting to burn the edge of my eyes. They were ready to escape as my hands trembled and my heart raced. My breathing was at a fast pace and my heart was aching.

I was scared to take another step just out of fear of the unknown. I didn't know what I was going to walk in on. I didn't know what I was going to witness and Lord knows I was scared.

"Grandma." My voice cracked and the tears that were dying to escape, slid down my face the moment I shut my eyes and approached my grandma's door that was shut closed.

She is ok. There is going to be a really good explanation for why the house is like this. Be positive. Everything is ok Kaizlyn. Breathe, I thought to myself as I placed my hand on the doorknob.

I stood there, not ready to accept whatever was about to be behind this door. I began to count down from ten and once I reached one, I closed my eyes then opened the door.

"Just the pppp...person I've been waiting to see." His voice caused my eyes to pop open.

My eyes began to dart around the room until they landed on my grandma who was tied to a chair. She had grey scotch tape on her mouth and wrapped around her arms and legs.

I could see the sorrow in her eyes as she looked at me. Her body was shaking and I had no clue as to what I should do.

"Why do you want? Why are you back here?" I questioned him, and he looked at me from side to side before he burst into laughter.

I began to ease towards my grandma because I thought that he wasn't paying attention but the moment I took a step, he pulled a gun from behind his back and pointed it at my grandma.

"Take one more step and I will kill her," he roared, and I dropped to my knees and began to cry and scream.

My body was shaking as I looked up at the man that was dressed in the same clothes that he had on the last time he was at our house, but this time his car wasn't outside. Which if it was, it would have alerted me and I would have called the cops.

"Why are you doing this?" I asked him as my voice shook and I held my knees up to my chest. "Please just let us go. What do you want, money?"

I didn't have money to give him, but I would sure as hell try my hardest to come up with it.

"Is that what you think?" He looked at me.

He then began to pace back and forth. He still had the gun in his hand as he carelessly moved it in any direction.

While he was in his own zone, I looked at my grandma. She now had tears in her eyes and I hated to see her tied up like that. I had to do something. There was no way that I was going to lose her to whoever this crazy person was.

"So, your grandma didn't tell you who I was?" He turned around quickly and looked at me.

Yes, me and her were supposed to talk about the shit, but we never did.

"No." I shook my head and he burst into a fit of laughter again.

"You ol' bitch. You never really liked me anyway," he rambled off.

"It was because of you that my father sent me off. I blame you. I fucking blame you. Y'all have no idea what I went through when y'all sent me to stay with them damn people. Do you know how it felt, to know that your own father didn't want you? Then to have to stay with a family that was just as ill as me?" He laughed as he scratched the side of his head with the gun.

I looked at him. Whoever he was and whatever he had been through had made him this way. I could tell that he had been through a lot and was battling with those demons every day. The way his clothes were filthy. The hair on his head was thick with little white fuzz balls inside of it. His eyes were blood-shot red and he twitched every now and again. Also, the way he was laughing right now, let me know that something was really wrong with him.

"Daisey, you know what the fuck happened to me?" he shouted as he looked over at my grandma who was crying so hard that she was choking up.

"My grandma's husband was beating and raping me. He was having his fucking way with me as many times as he wanted to, and you know? Nobody gave a fuck. They didn't believe me. You know why, because they already had it in their heads that I was sick. That I was mentally ill and that I was just sprouting out shit." He paused, looked up at the ceiling then he looked back at my grandma.

"But I guess that was my karma, huh?" He glared at my grandma.

"It was my fucking karma, huh bitch?" he shouted, which caused me to jump.

The scene before me was so intense, and I didn't know what exactly was the history between the two of them, but I don't think I wanted to know.

"Did your grandma ever tell you about me?" He looked at me.

"No, and I don't want to know you," I spat.

He chuckled and stumbled over to where my grandma was. I leaped to my feet and screamed, "Don't fucking touch her."

"Sit your ass down before I use this." He pointed the gun at me and I backed up.

When he reached my grandma, I wanted to run and go save her but I also didn't want to die.

Seconds later, he ripped the tape off of my grandma's mouth, causing her to scream in agony, and I had to gasp and cover my mouth because I knew it hurt.

"Daisey, are you going to tell her who I am or do I have to?" He looked at her in a creepy way as his head tilted from side to side, and I looked at my grandma.

"I'm sorry." Her voice trembled as she looked at me.

Now I was confused, scared and just wanted to be saved from this horror scene.

"Are you going to tell her or am I going to have to?" he asked again.

"Why.. why do you want her to know who you are? Did you forget what you did?" my grandma yelled at him, and a smirk appeared on his face.

He ran his hand down his face and then stared off at nothing in particular.

"How could I forget somebody as pretty as her? I could never forget her. I could never forget how she felt." He smiled widely as he reminisced about whatever they were talking about.

"You are a sick bastard," my grandma spat as she leaned forward and spit right on him.

"Run... Kaizlyn... just run," my grandma yelled in my direction.

"What? No, I'm not leaving you here with this man. I can't lose you. I already lost my mother," I cried. "I can't."

"Kaizlyn, listen to me. I will be ok." She nodded and I began to cry hard as hell as I debated on what I should do.

Shaking my head, I began to slowly walk backwards towards the door.

"Don't do it," he warned me.

I began to count down from five... 5, 4, 3, 2, 1.... I darted out of the room door, bumping into the wall on my way out.

"You bitch," I heard him yell at my grandma, and then I heard a big crash.

I wanted to go back, but I kept running until I got to the front door.

Pow!

He shot the gun and I looked back at him as I struggled to get out of the front door. Finally opening the door, I darted out of the house. The cool breeze hit my face as he let the gun go off again.

Pow!

"Don't run away from your father," he shouted out, and it was like my ears began to ring. I couldn't believe what I had just heard. I felt like I couldn't breathe and I felt like I was about to pass out as I ran across the grass and up the neighbor's house.

Banging on the door, I prayed that somebody answered before he made his way off of the porch.

"Let me in, please. Help!" I banged on the door and looked over my shoulder as he began to make his way off of the porch.

I was now scared for my life because I had no clue exactly what this man, who I now knew as my father, was capable of.

TO BE CONTINUED...

NOTE FROM THE AUTHOR

*H*ey my loves! Like Omg, we have another one. I still can't believe you all rock with me the way that you do. I swear, if I have never told you before, THANK YOU!! I appreciate every last one of you and I truly wish that I could tell you all individually. I hope that each and every last one of you enjoyed this read just as much as I did writing it. Please leave a review and let me know exactly what you thought. I love you all and I promise there is more to come.

xoxo- Prenisha Aja'

ABOUT THE AUTHOR

 Prenisha Aja' whom was born and raised in Conroe, Tx.

She's a 28 year old author who fell in love with the art of it all by picking up her first urban book decades ago. From writing down stories about her life in a journal to participating in the short story challenge that took Facebook by a storm, it all lead her to one thing. Being a Author!

With her foot in the door and not knowing much about the industry, she wrote and Self-Published her Debut Novel A Bitter Love which opened many doors for her.

Prenisha hopes to that her writing will keep you interested and wanting more which each book that she drops.

To keep up with all things Author Prenisha Aja', such as upcoming releases, sneak peeks, giveaways, and much more, join my readers group: bookwithHER

Royalty Publishing House is now accepting manuscripts from aspiring or experienced urban romance authors!

WHAT MAY PLACE YOU ABOVE THE REST:

Heroes who are the ultimate book bae: strong-willed, maybe a little rough around the edges but willing to risk it all for the woman he loves.

Heroines who are the ultimate match: the girl next door type, not perfect - has her faults but is still a decent person. One who is willing to risk it all for the man she loves.

The rest is up to you! Just be creative, think out of the box, keep it sexy and intriguing!

If you'd like to join the Royal family, send us the first 15K words (60 pages) of your completed manuscript to submissions@royaltypublishing-house.com

LIKE OUR PAGE!

Be sure to <u>LIKE</u> our Royalty Publishing House page on Facebook!

CPSIA information can be obtained
at www.ICGtesting.com
Printed in the USA
LVHW041723160419
614384LV00002B/202